LR
Tu

5/10

D1455365

JUDGMENT AT GOLD BUTTE

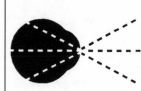

This Large Print Book carries the
Seal of Approval of N.A.V.H.

JUDGMENT AT GOLD BUTTE

TERRELL L. BOWERS

THORNDIKE PRESS
A part of Gale, Cengage Learning

Detroit • New York • San Francisco • New Haven, Conn • Waterville, Maine • London

GALE
CENGAGE Learning™

Copyright © 2008 by Terrell L. Bowers.
Thorndike Press, a part of Gale, Cengage Learning.

ALL RIGHTS RESERVED
All of the characters in this book are fictitious, and any resemblance to actual persons, living or dead, is purely coincidental.
Thorndike Press® Large Print Western.
The text of this Large Print edition is unabridged.
Other aspects of the book may vary from the original edition.
Set in 16 pt. Plantin.

LIBRARY OF CONGRESS CATALOGING-IN-PUBLICATION DATA

Bowers, Terrell L.
    Judgment at Gold Butte / by Terrell L. Bowers.
      p. cm. — (Thorndike Press large print western)
    ISBN-13: 978-1-4104-2013-8 (alk. paper)
    ISBN-10: 1-4104-2013-2 (alk. paper)
    1. Large type books. I. Title.
PS3552.O87324J84 2009
813'.54—dc22   2009034345

Published in 2009 by arrangement with Thomas Bouregy & Co., Inc.

Printed in Mexico
3 4 5 6 7 13 12 11 10

For my darling wife.
God smiled down on me when He
brought us together.

CHAPTER ONE

Born without a name, he started off in life as the unwanted offspring of a saloon gal known only as Joey. She would dance or sing and often worked customers for drinks. Not exactly chaste, she wasn't too particular about the kind of men in her life. "Joe" began to earn his keep almost from the time he could walk, cleaning spittoons and mopping up after drunks. A week after his seventh birthday, his mother contracted a fever and died. From the day they laid her to rest in the potter's field next to the regular cemetery, Joe began to work twelve to sixteen hours a day to eke out a meager existence.

The closest thing Joe had ever had to a father was an elderly gambler slowly being eaten away by consumption, who took Joe in when he was about twelve. Scholar Lund died some three years later, but he instilled in Joe a purpose for living and the desire to get ahead. The man equated life to a poker game — if a man wanted to succeed, he had to play his hand a little smarter than the next man. Scholar taught Joe many things during their short time together, but mainly how to make the most of the cards he was dealt.

Joe took on an early maturity that belied his youth and moved up from swamper to tending bar at eighteen. He learned to handle himself, often taking charge of rowdy customers or stopping a fight. By the time he was twenty-one, he was dealing faro and blackjack for the house. A few years later he was playing poker professionally and winning enough to earn a fair living.

Once Joe had mastered his craft, he began to move from city to city, often venturing to distant mining towns, wherever there was a high-stakes game. He honed his game and began to acquire a measure of prominence . . . until he crossed the path of Alan Masterson in the town of Pueblo, Colorado. That's when his luck took a turn for the worse.

Alan was a braggart and a bully, bigger than most, with a mouth that never quit. Having played cards with the man once, Joe knew better than to sit at his table a second time. This night, as soon as the man stormed into the casino, Joe had a notion he ought to pick up his chips and leave. He should have, but he didn't.

"Where's Lola?" Alan bellowed. His teeth were clenched in hate, and his face glowed red with fury. He grabbed the bartender by the front of the shirt and nearly dragged him over the counter. "Where's that filthy tramp?"

"Hold on, Mr. Masterson," the barkeep whimpered. "What's gotten into you?"

"I had a hundred dollars on me when I was dancing with her earlier. Now it's missing," Alan snarled. "That thieving little witch robbed me!"

The bartender shook his head. "It can't be, Mr. Masterson. We have strict rules about any of the girls' taking money. Lola has never been accused of trying to steal from a customer."

"You calling me a liar?" Alan demanded, pulling back a fist to strike the bartender.

"No! I didn't mean that, Mr. Masterson," the bartender blubbered, fearful of getting poked in his favorite nose. "We'll sure look into it. That's all I meant."

Alan was about to snarl back at him when he spotted Lola. She had the misfortune to return from a back room. She spied him and started to raise a hand in a wave until she saw the twisted rage on his face. Startled at his fury, she darted across the room to the stairs, a flash of fear paling her complexion.

Alan shoved men aside and bounded across the room to intercept her. The girl made it to the stairway, but before she could scramble up, Alan grabbed hold of her skirt and yanked her backward. Her feet went out from under her, and she landed hard on the wooden steps.

"You dirty little thief!" Alan roared. "I'll teach you to steal from me!"

"Alan, please!" she cried. "I don't know what you're talking about!"

But he was not in a listening mood. He slapped her with an open palm. Before she could cower or get her hands up to protect herself, he smacked her a second time.

Joe expected someone to step up and defend the girl, but not a man uttered a word to stop the bully.

"That's enough, Masterson!" he announced sternly, rising to his feet. "You touch that girl again, and I'll see how tough you are when it comes to mixing it up with a man."

Alan swore vehemently. "Stay out of this, tinhorn!" he sneered. "Lola's going to give back every dime she stole from me!"

Joe took a step toward the man. "I won't tell you again, tough guy. If you have a gripe, we'll send for a lawman and sort it out. No one mistreats a woman while I'm around."

Alan turned his back to the cowering woman and faced Joe. "I know your kind, Joe Bratt," he jeered. "You try playing the big man with me, and I'll blow a hole right through your pasteboard heart!"

"Best think this through, Masterson." Joe did not back down. "You've knocked Lola around enough for your lousy money."

Alan lowered his hand to his gun butt. "I'll let you know when I've gotten my money's worth, Bratt. I'm going to teach this slippery-fingered thief a lesson she won't ever forget."

"Lola will pay back whatever she took from you, Alan." A man Joe knew as Saul spoke up. "Give her a chance to surrender it."

"That's right," the bartender put in. "I'll see to it you get back every dime, Mr. Masterson. And if Lola did steal from you, we'll sure enough give her the boot out of town."

"I'm going to finish what I started," Alan vowed a second time, glaring at the group with a challenge burning in his red-rimmed

11

gaze. "If any one of you thinks you can stop me, make your move!"

"Last warning," Joe reiterated. "You're not going to touch the lady again."

But Alan was not willing to listen to reason. He grabbed for his gun, intent upon killing the gambler who dared try to stop him from his vengeful bloodlust.

Joe was not known as a gunfighter, but he had spent time with and gotten pointers from some of the best gunmen in the business. And he had done a fair amount of practicing.

Alan's gun came clear of leather and swept upward, the muzzle aligning at Joe's chest. Masterson managed to do everything quicker than Joe — except pull the trigger. Joe's gun went off first, and the bullet hit its mark.

The impact of the slug knocked Alan backward. As the gun slipped from his fingers, he fell on top of Lola. She squealed in surprise but managed to shove herself free. Alan's lifeless body tumbled to the bottom of the steps.

Saul, who was closest to the stairs, walked over to Alan. He knelt on the floor and examined the man as Joe holstered his pistol. When he rose back up, he shook his head. "Looks as if Masterson will no longer be casting the tallest shadow in town," he said.

"About time he got his due," the bartender declared, approaching to take a look at the fallen troublemaker. "It was only a matter of time."

Lola glanced down at the dead man and then turned to Joe. "I never took any money from him," she declared. "Honest! I never robbed anyone."

Saul patted the dead man's pockets and turned out his vest. "Here's his money!" he exclaimed. "The vest pocket has split a seam. The money slid in between the two layers of material. Stupid clod had the money all along and just didn't know it."

"I didn't want a gunfight," Joe explained, feeling the weight of responsibility for having killed a man. "I figured he would take me on with his fists. Once he went for his gun, he didn't leave me any choice."

Saul gave Joe a sympathetic look. "Fair fight or not, Bratt, you'd best light a fire under the tail of your horse. Alan is the son of Conroy Masterson, and that man swings a fair amount of weight here in town. He'll demand *you* swing at the end of a rope for killing his boy."

"But he forced the fight! He drew first."

"Won't make no difference to Conroy,"

13

the bartender agreed. "He's the mayor, and his brother-in-law owns half the county. Betwixt those two fellows, they'll sure enough figure a way to put the short end of a rope around your neck."

"Dad-gum!" Joe swore under his breath. "I sure don't favor the idea of being a wanted man."

"I and some of the others will testify to what happened on your behalf," Saul offered, "but I doubt it will be enough."

"Afraid Saul is right," the bartender put in. "A fast-talking, high-priced attorney might claim we were tired of being pushed around by Masterson. They could sure enough make it look like we were willing to condone a murder."

"Murder?" Joe was growing more concerned by the second. "I had no choice."

"Sorry, friend," Saul said, heaving a sigh. "The way Conroy is going to see it, this killing would have been self-defense only if Masterson had killed *you.*"

Joe didn't have to consider his options. There weren't any. He cashed in his chips, headed over to the livery, and saddled his horse. Within fifteen minutes he was riding along the back streets and working his way out of town. It had been a fair fight — a fight forced upon him because he'd befriended a helpless woman — but it didn't matter. Joe Bratt was now a wanted man.

Raylene Stanfield tipped her bonnet forward on her head to shield her eyes from the sun. She tasted grit between her teeth and waved a hand in front of her face, a futile attempt to keep from inhaling a cloud of powdery dust raised from the churning hooves of the team. Several hot and dusty days on the trail and she was wondering about the sanity of making such a journey. The trip from the outskirts of Denver to the mountainous region known as the Sangre de Cristo Range seemed to take forever. Worse, she had considerable misgivings about their destination.

The team plodded at a slow pace, while the wagon creaked and bounced along the rutted trail. Not as large as a Conestoga, the covered wagon was shorter and less durable than the mighty prairie schooners that crossed the open plains. Being lightweight and compact, the rig was easily drawn by a single team of horses, but it offered little physical comfort.

"Gracious, Father!" Raylene exclaimed, clinging to the wagon seat with both hands. "I very much doubt we have missed a single bump or rut since we left Denver!"

15

"Not the best of trails, I admit, but this shortcut will save us five miles. The stage-coach route should be just over the next rise," her parent reassured her. "Once we're on the main trail, the ride will be much smoother."

"I still don't understand why you couldn't get an assignment in a more civilized place," she complained. "Surely Gold Butte wasn't the only town in need of a judge."

"Are the sheep of the hills not as important as the sheep in the valley?"

Raylene sighed. "You and your parables, Father. I sometimes wonder if you think of me as one of your lost sheep, instead of a real person."

He laughed the way he always laughed at her discord. Raylene had a great respect for her father. He was a good man with a good heart and a desire to be of service to others. But he had a habit of ignoring her opinion or not even listening to what she had to say. Raylene was a dutiful daughter, having taken on the chores of cook and house-keeper when her mother died. The years had slipped away, and she had chosen to stay with her father, becoming his aid, his clerk, his confidante.

As for entertaining suitors or finding a husband to share her life with, what man could measure up to her father? He was a pillar without equal, known for his fairness and devotion to the law. Her attitude about seeking his equal had driven most admirers away.

"In truth, my daughter," her father interrupted her deliberation, "I have always wanted to tackle a position of this type. I've no desire to be a big-city judge, going through the same mundane drudgery day after day — petty theft, an occasional fight, the endless stream of people wanting to sue over something trivial. Is that all there is to being a judge?"

"Yes, but do you really want a wild and unsettled town like Gold Butte?" Raylene asked. "You said they have their own kangaroo court system and that some rowdies drove out the last two judges sent there. It has no school or church, no organized social structure whatsoever. It sounds like a very hostile place."

"My point exactly," he replied. "Who needs a firm hand more than an untamed town filled with corruption and criminals? I'm sure there are also good people there who need the civilization real justice can bring to their town. We will settle mining disputes, perhaps prevent a range war, put the lawless behind bars, and perform dozens of other needed tasks. This is the position I have yearned for all my life, a place where we can start from scratch and construct a healthy, law-abiding community. I tell you, my daughter, this is all I've dreamed about since I earned my law degree. It's my calling, my destiny." He reached over and patted her on the knee. "My life's ambition will be fulfilled if we can accomplish this."

Raylene heaved a sigh of inward resignation. "I understand, Father. You wish to make a difference" — she flashed a smile at him — "and that is the reason I am here at your side. I want to make a difference as well."

"That's my girl," he chirped merrily. "We'll be the guiding servants of the people, working for the good of the community and helping to build a fine town with a firm moral foundation. I won't be a judicial puppet for the rich and powerful; we'll make Gold Butte a better place to live." His face brightened with inspiration. "I feel it in my bones, darling daughter — this post is going to be the culmination of our life's work together."

She smiled at his enthusiasm, reminded of why she had stuck by him these many years. Perhaps she would find her own destiny in Gold Butte. Who could say what —

There came a sudden *crack,* the sound of wood giving way. At nearly the same instant a wheel at the front of the wagon splintered, and the corner collapsed.

Raylene and her father were thrown to the low side, while the team jumped and lurched forward, spooked by the unexpected shift of weight and her father's erratic jerk on the reins.

The vicious motion threw her father off balance. He teetered backward and then, with a second violent jerk of the wagon, was tossed forward over the front rail. Raylene managed to hold on to the wagon seat with one hand and made a desperate grab for her father's jacket. The cloth slipped through her fingers, and he disappeared headfirst over the front of the wagon as the frightened team of horses recklessly bolted.

The wagon lunged forward, tilted crazily to one side, and was dragged a short way until the remaining front wheel slammed into a large rock. The boulder stopped the wagon with such bone-jarring abruptness, the trace was ripped loose from the wagon tongue. The frightened team dashed away, running wild, still in harness, pulling the dislodged singletree behind them. The horses quickly vanished over the hill, leaving only a trail of dust behind.

Raylene gathered her wits and pushed herself upright. She frantically searched over the front railing for her father. He was not visible below or to either side of the wagon bed. Climbing quickly down to the ground, she spied the twisted body lying on the road some thirty feet beyond the rear of the wagon. It appeared her father had been run over.

Joe reached the crest of the hill and paused to take a careful look around. That's when something hit him hard between the shoulders. A second later he heard the echo of a far-off gunshot. He groaned from the shock of being hit and caught sight of the smoke from a distant rifleman. The shooter was among a group of riders.

Conroy's posse!

Joe ducked low over the saddle and dug his heels into his steed's ribs as a dozen guns started blasting away at him. As his mount raced over the top of the hill, Joe felt a searing pain spread between his shoulders, felt the warm dampness of blood trickling down his back. One of the posse had been a good shot . . . or very lucky. He had hit Joe from a long way off.

Horses were one thing Joe knew almost as well as cards. His mare was half Arabian but had the stamina of a Morgan. She was long on bottom with both speed and endurance. She used that stamina now, putting distance between him and the armed party. By the time Joe reached the timberline, he was a mile in front of his pursuers.

Once concealed among the trees, he picked up an animal trail and began to work his way upward. Having traveled this route before, he remembered there was a rock plateau hidden deep within the mountain range. If he could reach that mesa, he would be able to lose any but the best of trackers. With luck, none of those in the hunting party was that good at following a man.

Winding along the narrow, meandering trail, he gave thought to which direction to take when he reached the plateau. If the posse split up, they could cover the trails to both the east and west. If he went straight ahead, it meant following the railroad and riding through sizable towns. The men behind him might have sent messages by rail or over the telegraph to alert the people along that route. He couldn't play hide-and-seek in the hills; he had to find out how badly he was hurt.

Reaching up to the back of his neck, he gingerly explored the wound. The bullet had obviously lost much of its punch from being fired at such a long distance. There was considerable bleeding, and he could feel a slight bulge from the slug in his left shoulder blade. He'd been lucky. Had the shooter been using a buffalo gun, he would be dead now. However, even if he were a medical doctor, he couldn't reach up between his shoulders to treat the wound. He was going to need some help.

His first inclincation was to ride toward cattle country, where a farmer or rancher might patch him up. The problem with that option was the posse would also see it as his most likely choice, which meant Joe had to do the unexpected. He knew of a mining town, Gold Butte, well off the main trails. While there might be a telegraph there, it was a pretty wild place, with the only law being men hired by the mine owners. He would make for Gold Butte and try to locate a doctor. With any luck, the posse would not expect him to try and hole up in a nearby town.

The pain between his shoulders wasn't severe, but he could feel the warm spread of blood seeping down his back. He worried that he might pass out from loss of blood, but he had to put distance between himself and the posse. He clenched his jaw firmly and remained focused on his escape route. He had to keep his wits about him long enough to reach help.

Gordon Stanfield's head rested on Raylene's lap. She stared down at him through tear-misted eyes. The wheel had run over one leg, but the real damage had been done by his awkward landing. It appeared he had broken his neck in the fall. Her father had died without uttering a single cry.

She prayed softly over his body and then sobbed against his lifeless chest. After a short while she regained her composure and sniffed back her tears.

"It's so unfair!" She voiced her despair. Her father had been on the verge of fulfilling his final dream. What a cruel fate to die en route to his destiny.

A feeling of helpless frustration fought to displace her hurt over the loss of the best man she had ever known. He had been her guiding light, her inspiration. Now he was gone, snatched from her by a broken wheel and a tragic fall from their wagon. She mourned not only for the end of a virtuous man's life but also for the fact that his work was left unfinished, his legacy incomplete.

Gordon could have had any number of appointments, but he'd volunteered to sit on the bench and dispense law at Gold

Butte. Even though the town posed an enormous challenge for any judge, she knew he would have succeeded where others had tried and failed. Gold Butte was reputed to be a community of lawless mine and cattle barons, with odious saloons and wicked casinos filled with a multitude of hardcase miners, rowdy cowboys, and more than a few poor souls trying to scratch out a living.

I should have been born a man!

Raylene had always enjoyed being a part of her father's world. She would have been elated to sit on the bench and determine who was in the wrong or who should pay for a crime. But being a judge was a man's duty, so she had had to be satisfied to act as a recorder and clerk for her father, sitting in his court, taking notes, and learning to comprehend his decisions. She had been more than a secretary, as he often relied on her objective perspective before making a ruling, always concerned that his choice be fair and impartial. Along with her duties at the court, she had kept the house, prepared the meals, done laundry, and been steadfast in supporting her father. She had been proud to be a part of his work for the good of mankind. After being a circuit judge for so many years, he had taken a job where he truly could make a difference. And she would have been a part of his dream.

Now those notions were lost; her father lay dead before her.

The sound of approaching horses diverted her attention to the road. A man on horseback had a lead rope attached to her father's team. He had evidently found the animals wandering up the trail and was returning them to their owner.

Raylene gave a final loving look at her father and stood up. She hurriedly brushed at her tears and lifted a hand to greet the stranger.

"Over here!" she called out, waving her arms to attract his attention.

The man drew closer, and Raylene could make him out more clearly. He appeared a bit taller than average and somewhat older than her own twenty-five years. His complexion was rather pale, but the dark suit and hat he wore, although dusty from travel, appeared to be expensive and fit him nicely.

"I found this here team about a half mile up the beaten path, munching some buffalo grass," he explained. "I could see by their tracks, they didn't come from the main trail, so I backtracked them this way." He looked past her to the body of her father and gave a solemn shake of his head.

"Damn. I was afraid someone might have

had an accident."

"Yes," she replied gravely. "We lost a wheel, and my father fell under the wagon. He's . . ." She had to swallow a sob to get out the word. "Dead."

A look of compassion flooded the man's face. "I'm real sorry, ma'am."

Raylene turned to other immediate problems. "Even if the team hadn't run off, I'm sure I wouldn't have been able to repair the wagon by myself. There's a spare wheel stored under the bed of the wagon, but I don't know what shape it's in."

"Maybe I can lend a hand," he offered.

"I'm beholden to you for your help, Mr. . . . ?"

"Joe Bratt."

"I'm Raylene Stanfield, Mr. Bratt. And I thank you for returning our horses."

Joe Bratt climbed down from his horse and tied off the team. After securing his own mount, he walked over to the wagon. The man looked fit, Raylene noted, but he moved about as stiffly as a wooden soldier.

"Won't be much of a chore to rehitch the team to the wagon," he advised her after a short examination. "As for the axle, it don't appear to be bent or twisted out of shape. If we can get your spare wheel on, you should be able to reach the next town."

26

Joe backed up a step but didn't offer to retrieve the spare wheel. Raylene bit back a remark about his not being much of a gentleman and got down on her hands and knees. She crawled under the wagon bed and located the wheel. She had to lie on her back to unlash it from its storage place. Then she let it down one edge at a time and pushed and dragged it out into the open. She reminded herself to appreciate the fact that Joe Bratt had returned her team and stopped to help, but he certainly lacked gallantry. He continued to stand idly by the front of the wagon while she rose to her feet and dusted herself off. Bending over, she took hold of the wheel and lifted the rim, standing it upright. Next, she tugged and grunted, rolling the wheel to the front of the wagon, where she worked it back until it was lined up with the axle. Once it was in place, she stopped to regain her wind.

"Won't we need to build us a lever to elevate the wagon?" she asked.

Joe lifted the corner a couple inches and announced, "Seems the weight is evenly spread, so I ought to able to raise it by myself."

Raylene arched her spine to relieve the ache from being stooped over, while Joe put his back to the front of the wagon and removed his jacket. She noticed he seemed more ashen than before and wondered if he was upset at seeing a dead body.

"I've got maybe one good lift in me," he said. "You'll need to have the wheel ready to push into place quick as you can."

"Of course," she said, still a little miffed at the man's laziness. "I helped my father do this once before."

Joe bent his knees, laced his fingers under the edge of the wagon bed, and took a deep breath. "Whenever you're ready," he said.

Raylene scooted the wheel around until it was as close as she could get it to the axle. She planted her feet for leverage and took a firm hold on the rim.

"I'm ready," she declared.

Joe lifted, groaning from the strain. He looked capable of doing the job, but he didn't seem to be as strong as her father. No sooner had he gotten the axle up off the ground than his knees began to tremble.

"Hurry!" was the only word he said.

Raylene quickly worked the wheel back and forth to get it closer. "A little higher," she instructed. "Just a couple more inches!"

Joe grunted again from the effort and managed to lift the wagon upward a bit more.

Raylene lined up the hub and shoved the wheel into place. "There!" she cried. "We got it!"

Joe let go . . . and collapsed.

For a moment Raylene thought he was pulling a prank, making light of actually doing a little hard work. Then she saw the dark crimson stain on the back of his shirt.

"What on earth?" she said.

Quickly dropping to her knees, she pulled the material back from his collar far enough to see an ugly puncture wound between his shoulders.

"My dear Lord!" she cried. "Mr. Bratt, you've been shot!"

CHAPTER TWO

Among some of her odd jobs when her father was not riding circuit, Raylene had helped tend to sick or injured people. She was not a nurse, but she had worked at a couple of town and city hospitals. She could see that the bullet had struck the base of Joe's neck at an odd angle and was embedded in the flesh near his shoulder blade. The wound itself didn't appear life-threatening, but he had lost a considerable amount of blood.

Raylene had seen gunshot victims before, but never had she been forced to perform the necessary surgery to remove the bullet. Luckily, she determined that the piece of lead was not set too deeply. She collected a blanket, rolled him onto it, and removed his shirt. Next, she used a small kitchen knife to gently work the piece of lead to the surface. Once it was out, she washed away the blood and cleansed the wound. Satisfied she had done the best she could, she folded a bit of cloth over the puncture and wrapped a bandage about his shoulder and neck to secure it in place.

Joe was not fully conscious, but Raylene roused him enough that he could cooperate with climbing into the wagon. He sagged onto her bed, facedown, and was instantly asleep from exhaustion and his injury.

Raylene left the man to rest and turned to other chores. First off, she located a shady spot and scooped out a grave for her father. Once she had buried him, she topped the site with a blanket of rocks to prevent animals from digging. She selected a couple of thick scrub-oak branches and used an ax to cut and trim them to usable lengths. Using a short piece of twine, she fashioned the two boughs into a cross and stuck it into the ground to mark her father's grave. Then she stood at the foot of his grave, lowered her head, and said a prayer.

She suffered from an overwhelming feeling of loss. Gordon had been the driving force in her life ever since she could remember. She couldn't imagine going on without him. Her heart was heavy with grief, and her future, which had always been tied to her father's work, was now in doubt. After a while she pulled herself together emotionally and walked away from his final resting place. There were chores that needed tending to.

The sun nestled against the distant horizon by the time Raylene had picketed the team and Joe's horse. She then rounded up wood for a fire. She didn't feel like eating, but she had an injured man to look after. It gave her purpose, a reason to keep going. Staying busy helped to stave off her sorrow and the tremendous sense of being alone.

With a fire crackling, she crept into the wagon to check on her patient. Joe seemed to be sleeping peacefully. Sitting back on her heels, she wondered if she should prepare some broth or simply heat a can of beans. That's when she heard horses on the trail. They came to a stop at her wagon, so she took Joe's gun from its holster and peeked out the back. It was dusk, but she made out four men — dusty, tired-looking riders mounted on lathered horses.

"Evening, missy," the leader of the group greeted her. "We're part of a posse from Pueblo, on the trail of a desperado. We lost his trail a couple hours back, but we're pretty sure he was wounded."

"A desperado?" she repeated, displaying immediate alarm. "What did he do?"

"Well, he kilt a man in a gunfight." The

man shrugged. "If it was up to me, I'd have called it self-defense and given him a pat on the back, but it was the mayor's son he kilt." The speaker showed his teeth in a grin. "Some folks get almighty touchy when you up and kill one of their kin."

Raylene placed the gun on the blankets and gave an affirmative nod. "Yes," she agreed, "there are those who believe they are entitled to retribution beyond what a judge and jury would allow."

"Durned if you don't sound downright judicial, ma'am."

"My father is a judge."

"Well, have you seen anyone on the road in the past few hours?" he asked. "The guy would have been alone and was dressed as something of a dude."

"I haven't seen anyone," she lied, fearful her soul would immediately be summoned to perdition.

The man glanced over at her team and the extra horse. "He was riding a big mare — looked a lot like that one in your string."

"My father is a circuit judge," she clarified. "His work requires us to travel a great deal."

The man smiled. "There's a few places out here the law ain't never been — that's a fact."

"It's my belief that wherever man is, law must follow, or chaos will," she stated.

"Yes, ma'am," he allowed graciously. "Spoken like the daughter of a judge."

"I believe I will take that as a compliment," she replied.

He bobbed his head and turned back to their business. "Well, like I said, one of the boys is pretty certain he hit the guy with a round from his Winchester, so he probably crawled into a hole to die."

"How dreadful!" she exclaimed.

When she offered nothing more, he asked, "Maybe your father saw the man we're looking for, ma'am?"

"No," she said a bit too quickly, but then recovered. "We were on our way to Gold Butte and had an accident. My father was killed." She gestured toward the fresh grave. "My . . . brother was banged up some too. He's resting here in the back of the wagon."

"Rough-and-tumble, wide-open town, Gold Butte," the man said, not doubting she was telling him the truth. "I hope you have a stout heart, ma'am. I don't think there's more than a few decent folks in the entire town."

"Thank you for the warning," she said.

"I'm sorry for your loss and wish you the best of luck." He tipped his hat and spoke to the others. "Let's go, men. That jasper couldn't have gotten far."

Raylene watched them ride away. As soon as they were out of sight, she sank down onto her knees and tried to slow the beating of her heart. She had lied to a posse! Harboring a fugitive was a serious offense. Why had she done it?

She stared over her shoulder at the shadowy form lying beneath the blankets of her bed.

"I wonder," she murmured, "if fate had a hand in sending you to me."

Joe thought he heard a soft voice and opened his eyes. From somewhere behind him there came a dim glimmer of light. He started to lift his head to look around, but a sudden pain caused him to pause. He tested his muscles and felt the tightness of a bandage that was wrapped about his shoulders and upper chest. He became aware of being in a bed, but it didn't smell like an ordinary bunk. There was a sweet fragrance on the pillow, the scent he sometimes noticed on a woman who had recently washed her hair.

"Are you awake?" a feminine voice asked.

Joe managed to cock his head to one side. As his faculties began to return, he recognized the woman he had helped with the wagon wheel. The light from a solitary lamp bathed her face in a warm glow. Not a strikingly beautiful woman, she was nonetheless wholesome and pleasant to behold. Her hair was pulled up tightly under a Quaker-style bonnet. Her cheeks were tear-streaked, and a deep sadness lay within her eyes. The sorrowful look reminded him of her father's death and the wagon mishap.

"Reckon I've been a heap of trouble to you, ma'am," he said hoarsely.

"Not at all," she replied. "Your arrival was a blessing."

He offered up a tight grin. "First time I've ever been accused of being a blessing."

"If it's not too presumptuous of me to ask, what is your profession, Mr. Bratt?"

"I'm a gambler by trade."

"A gambler?" She wrinkled her brow in disapproval. "What a horrible line of work."

"Maybe so, ma'am, but it keeps me from going hungry."

Joe got his arms under his body and gingerly pushed himself upward. The girl was quickly at his side, helping him to turn around and sit up. The effort caused him to grunt against the stiffness in his shoulders, but his head was clear. He decided the bullet wound must not have done any real damage.

"Didn't your parents warn you of the evils of gambling?" the woman asked.

"Never knew who my real father was," he admitted. "As for my mother, well" — he gave a shake of his head — "she didn't have a lot of time for teaching me much of anything. About the only one who ever took a shine to me was a gambler named Scholar, who kind of raised me for a few years."

"But you're a grown man. Once you were old enough to be on your own, didn't you ever want to amount to something? You could have become a farmer or rancher — even a lawman or teacher."

"The only contact I've had with lawmen over the years is when they were asking me to leave town or settling a dispute over some card slick trying to cheat. As for teachers, Scholar — the man who took me in — was the only real educated man I ever knew personally. And as for working the fields or riding herd on someone else's cattle, it never held much interest for me."

"Oh."

The woman sounded disappointed. Joe didn't know what to say, so he waited for her to speak again.

"Regardless of your background and lack of suitable ambition, I believe you are a good person, Mr. Bratt," she stated.

Joe frowned at the assertion. "What do you mean by 'good'?"

"I mean, unless you've killed other men before the one in Pueblo . . . ?"

Joe could not hide his surprise. "How do you know about the man in Pueblo?"

"A posse came by looking for you. The leader said you had killed a man, but he readily admitted it was in self-defense."

"Yes, ma'am, it was."

"What about before?" She continued to grill him with questions. "Are you a thief? Do you cheat the people you come into contact with? Do you drink to excess and use profanity? Do you smoke, chew, spit, and chase after women of . . . dubious honor?"

Joe chuckled. " *'Dubious honor'?* Don't reckon I ever heard it put quite that way before."

"Would you please answer my questions?"

He gave her a long look. She reminded him of a lady cardsharp he had met one time. She could bluff with the best of them and never gave away her hole card. After sitting in on one game with her, he had never again played against a woman.

"Why do you want to know so much about me?" He turned the questioning toward her. "I'm not in the habit of spouting my worth or faults to every stranger I come across."

"I have a proposition for you, but I must first determine if you are worthy."

"A proposition?"

"Yes, and remember, I saved you from the posse."

Joe tried to hunch his shoulders a bit . . . and it hurt. "Ow!" he said, uttering a groan. "That ain't the right way to be moving just yet."

"*Ain't* is not a proper word," she told him. "Do you think you could eliminate it from your vocabulary?"

"I didn't know there was anything wrong with the word," he said honestly.

"Mr. Bratt, I would like to believe you are an honorable man," the woman continued. "You were on the run from the law, but you still took time to stop and aid a traveler in distress. You were wounded, yet you said nothing. You helped me with the wheel and never asked for money or even my thanks. That tells me you have a good heart."

"Listen, lady." Joe decided to put a stop to her bragging on him. "I'm a man who makes his living playing cards. You asked about my parents, but I never had no real parents. Take my name — Joe Bratt. That's what I was called growing up. My mother's name was Josephine, but everyone called her Joey — women in her line of work don't have last names. I was her kid, so everyone called me Joey's brat. I latched on to Joe as a first name and took *brat* for the last name I didn't have. Scholar told me I should spell the name with two *t*'s so it would be more of a real name.

"You asked if I was a good man. Well, I don't cheat at cards to win, but I will take advantage of another man's weakness. I can read most men and can usually tell when they're holding good cards or trying to bluff. It gives me an advantage, and I use it."

"Then you are an honest man."

"So long as you don't ask what my hole card is."

"Mr. Bratt" — she gazed at him intensely — "what would you think about changing your name?"

"Do what?"

"How would you like to become Judge Gordon Stanfield?"

It was an outrageous idea, but one Raylene felt could work. Joe was running from the law and could use a new identity, while she desperately wanted to fulfill her father's dream. She knew the law in most out-of-the-way towns was little more than vigilante justice. If Joe was willing to be her mouthpiece, she could finish what her father had started.

Joe displayed no enthusiasm about the idea. "You want me to pretend to be a judge?" He grimaced. "Did you maybe miss the part where I told you how I ain't never been on the best of terms with the law? About the only thing I ever learned in court was not to argue with the judge. I ain't got the first idea how to sit before a bunch of strangers and dictate the law to them."

Raylene was not dissuaded. "I would teach you what to say, and I would be there to coach you whenever you had to rule on a difficult case. I took notes and consulted with my father ever since I learned to read and write. I know more about the law than a dozen lawyers combined."

"If you're so all-fired eager to do this, why not become a gavel-thumper yourself?"

"Because my father received the appointment, and I'm a woman. They don't appoint female judges. The people would never accept me, especially those in a mining town."

Joe gave his head a negative shake. "If the dealing out of justice is all that's important, what difference does it matter who sits on the throne?"

"A king sits on a throne," she corrected him. "A judge sits on a bench."

"The couple I've seen sat on chairs, not benches."

Raylene felt her patience wane. "Calling the chair a bench is merely symbolic. It really makes no difference if the judge is seated on a throne, a chair, a bench, or a saddle!"

"If you say so."

"And most of the law you need to know is common sense. You say you can read a man by studying him. If that is the case, you would make a fine judge. You could tell if a man was lying, and real justice is mostly about learning the truth."

"It still seems to me that you ought to be the one doing the judging."

"Would you vote for a woman sheriff?" she challenged. "How about for town mayor?"

"Well, I never gave it much thought. I've never voted for anyone before."

"There may come a day when a woman is accepted on the judicial bench, but it will be many years before that happens. I can't wait that long. The position is open right now, the one my father was to fill."

"Okay, so your only problem is being a

woman," he replied. "If you recall, I'm on the run from a posse. If someone found out you managed to stick me on a bench to deal out justice, you'd get tossed into jail right alongside me!"

"The leader of the posse said you acted in self-defense."

"I did," Joe said. "The fellow drew down on me and would have killed me if I hadn't been the quicker one to get off the first shot."

"I believe you."

"Too bad this here ain't a courtroom and you the presiding judge," Joe said sarcastically. "My troubles would all be over."

"Your past is not at issue. It is your future at stake, Mr. Bratt. I think you have a good heart, and this would give you a chance to mend your ways and become a decent man."

"Decent?" He was cynical. "How can pretending to be a judge be decent?"

"It would only be for a short while. Our goal is to settle local disputes, sort out mining claims, and incorporate law and order into the community. Once everything is operating smoothly, I will send word to the governor that you have resigned, and he can fill the post with a replacement judge."

"Why is this so blamed important?" Joe asked. "What difference does it make who

43

organizes the town?"

"It was my father's dream," she said softly. "It would have made his life's work complete."

"His dream," Joe repeated. "What about your own dreams?"

"Gold Butte is reputed to be a den of vice and criminal behavior," she told him curtly. "My single objective is to offer help to those who seek a better way of life. I have watched my father doing the job all my life. He has helped hundreds of people by dispensing justice. His mission was to bring order out of anarchy. There are people suffering at Gold Butte, people who need a man of good character to oversee the trouble there, help solve labor disputes, and put an end to crime."

"I'm nothing like your father," Joe replied. "I don't know how to help any of those people."

"You've lived on your own all of your life, used your wits to stay alive, and grown to be a man. Is that all you want? Is being a gambler enough?"

"It's all I know."

"I lied for you a few hours ago," she admitted. "I haven't lied to anyone in years, and never to a representative of the law."

That had an impact on Joe. He owed this

gal a debt. She had patched him up, given him a bed to sleep in — her bed — and had even sent the posse on their way, while hiding him in the back of her wagon.

"I've lived only for myself since I was a kid, ma'am, but I do have standards. I never cheat an honest man, never do harm to a woman or child, and I ain't never owed a debt that I didn't pay."

"Do we have a deal?"

"How long do you reckon I'd have to play this game you've got in mind before I break even with the house?"

"I shouldn't think it would take longer than three months to complete our task," she said. At his furrowed brow, she hurriedly finished. "Whether or not we succeed in bringing order to Gold Butte in that length of time, we will call it quits and go our separate ways."

"Three months, huh?" He appeared wary and indecisive. "Doing nothing but solving local disputes and sorting out the bad guys — that's all you want from me?"

"Yes."

Joe gave his head a negative shake. "Even if I agreed to your crazy scheme, I wouldn't be any good at it. I don't know enough about the law."

Raylene changed the subject. "Mr. Bratt,

why did you stop running from the posse long enough to bring the team of horses back here?"

"I figured someone was in trouble."

"What did that matter? You didn't know who was in trouble, and it could have meant your getting caught by that posse."

"I dunno," he said. "It just seemed like the right thing to do."

"See?" She flashed a triumphant smile. "That's exactly what I'm talking about! You claim not to know the law, yet you automatically did the right and decent thing. Sitting on the bench and dispensing justice is doing just that."

"Yeah?" Joe remained skeptical. "What if I had to rule on a killing or bank robbery? Being that I wouldn't be a real judge, and providing they have a local jail, I could maybe deal with small complaints. But I couldn't sentence anyone who committed a serious crime to the state prison. And if I ordered everyone hanged who offends the law, I'd end up tarred and feathered, then get hanged myself!"

"If a serious situation should arise, we can deal with it by issuing a Change of Venue. That means the trial would have to be held someplace else," Raylene explained.

Joe studied her for a moment. "You've got

all the answers, don't you?"

"Do we have a deal?"

Joe uttered a sigh. "Seems a high price for merely saving my hide."

"You did say you always repaid your debts."

"Yeah, big mouth that I've got, I did say that," Joe admitted. "As I'm still looking at a noose for killing a man in self-defense, I reckon I'll throw in with you. They can only hang me once."

Raylene gave him a quick hug. "You won't regret it," she said cheerfully, pulling back to smile at him. "I promise."

Gold Butte was a substantial town with a sizable mining operation and several nearby ranches. A narrow-gauge railroad spur had been built, which ran from a cooperative loading dock down to the railhead. There were two kinds of narrow-gauge railways built throughout the mining country. The first had rails three feet apart — ideal for maneuvers in the constricted canyons and for moving ore to the main railroad line, where it could be off-loaded onto larger cars and shipped to a smelter. This surface railway also allowed for supplies to be shipped from a distant station, rather than hauled by the more expensive freight and express companies. The second kind was used inside tunnels and often powered by mules or strong men, operating underground in mine shafts for moving ore, waste debris, or even transporting workers to different locations.

As Joe surveyed the town's rail spur, he slipped his freshly laundered coat jacket back and removed the thong from his gun, making it ready for instant use. Raylene had wanted him to discard his gun, but Joe had been in a fair number of these wild and lawless towns. To be without his gun would have been like riding in without any trousers.

They entered slowly, taking time to look over Gold Butte. They saw a number of large, central wooden buildings, while the housing for the miners and other residents ran from rows of shacks to scattered tents and wagons. Three saloons, a couple of eating emporiums, and several stores lined the mud-rutted main street. As it was midday, most of the men were working, so there were only a few people on the street.

"We were promised a place to live." Raylene spoke up. "The letter said it used to be a church until the preacher about starved and decided to leave town."

They had already passed the livery at the

edge of town, complete with a blacksmith sign and a smoking forge. A little farther up the road was a second barn.

"I 'spect the town couldn't support two stables, ma'am," he told Raylene, tipping his head in that direction. "If I'm not mistaken, it looks as if there's a cross painted on that big building there on the left side of the street."

"A barn?" Raylene's voice revealed her dismay. "The lodging for a respected judge is a barn?"

"Can't tell the cards by looking at the backside, ma'am." Joe attempted some comfort. "It's likely real comfy inside."

"Quite so," Raylene replied, immediately firming her resolve. "Let's have a look at our new home."

Joe had to admit, the gal at his side had pluck. She had buried her father and gone about his business without hesitation. She was brave and determined, but he feared her plan was doomed to fail.

Joe guided the team to the front of the barn and pulled them to a stop. Sure enough, someone had painted a white cross above the loft. A cooked sign, which had once borne the name of the church, was posted on the side of the building, but someone had splashed red paint over most of the lettering. Instead of barn doors, the front had been converted into a wall with a normal-sized entry.

"It appears the gospel wasn't real popular hereabouts," Joe said.

"I doubt a justice of the peace will be any better received," she cautioned.

"Some folks have a real dislike for any kind of law, ma'am. I've a feeling this job is going to be like crawling around on all fours, blindfolded, in a field of bear traps."

"You mustn't call me *ma'am*," Raylene scolded him. "You're going to have to pose as my brother. Either address me as Raylene or as your sister."

"I don't know how to behave like your brother."

"Well, you're hardly old enough to pretend to be my father."

Joe showed a silly grin. "Mayhap we could pretend we're man and wife."

Raylene bore into him with a hard gaze. "You are a gentleman, remember?"

"I've been accused of worse things."

"I explained it all to you on the way here: your name is Gordon Stanfield," she reminded him curtly. "You have been a circuit judge for three years, but this is your first permanent assignment."

"Three years don't sound like much."

"We can't very well say you've been on the bench for twenty years." She told him the obvious. "No one is going to question you — not if you follow my instructions."

"Yes, ma'am."

Raylene groaned. "Call me Ray or Raylene."

Joe cleared his throat. "I ain't never called no proper lady by her first name."

"You have my permission."

"I'll give it a go, but it ain't going to sound natural-like."

Raylene expelled another sigh of frustration. "And please try to stop using the word *ain't!*"

Before Joe could reply, they were interrupted.

"Good day to you folks!" a cheerful voice said.

They rotated in the wagon seat to see a man and woman approach, smiles of greeting on their faces.

The lady was nicely attired in a modest dress, with her hair pulled into a bun at the back of her head. She was on the matronly side but still a handsome woman. As for the man, he was of average height, attired in a clean black suit and matching felt hat — one of those Joe considered a city type, capped with a round dome and sporting a rather narrow brim. It was constructed for fashion, not to shelter a man from the sun. The gent had a groomed mustache and showed a set of fairly straight teeth when he smiled.

"We've been keeping watch for you every day for the past week." He greeted them like lost relatives. "I'm Tom Lawson, the mayor of Gold Butte, and this is my wife, Ellen."

Raylene was obviously used to this sort of thing. She flashed a dazzling smile and immediately oozed a sweetness that could have coerced an entire hive of worker bees from their queen.

"It's a pleasure to make your acquaintance," she said. "This is my brother, the Honorable Gordon Stanfield. I'm Raylene."

Ellen stepped over to speak directly to Raylene. At the same time, the mayor came around to the opposite side of the wagon to confront Joe. He reached upward with an outstretched hand.

"We appreciate your coming, Judge. If I might say so, the town is sorely in need of you. We have a sheriff and a couple deputies, but they're more of a problem than a solution. We need an honest man to sort out the misdeeds and crime we're dealing with. Gold Butte has some good people, but there are rough customers around who prefer to keep the town untamed."

Joe shook Tom Lawson's hand and glanced up the street to see that a few men had gathered at the front of one of the saloons. There appeared to be some interest in the new arrivals in town. "You say the sheriff is not exactly a straight shooter?"

"He follows orders from the richest and most powerful men in town, the Estcott brothers. The law here does keep the peace, but it also enforces a heavy taxation on every business in town."

"Taxes are what support the local government," Joe replied, trying to sound judge-like.

"Yes, but since Sheriff Unger was put into power, there has been no one to speak for the little guy. If one of the miners, ranchers, or a business owner has a grievance, it's pretty much swept aside and ignored. Step on the toes of one of the select few, and it means a beating or worse." Tom gave a helpless shrug. "Guess you probably know something about the problems, because the two previous judges have quit the position and moved on. Neither of them lasted a month."

"Sometimes when the deck is stacked and the house is holding all the chips, a man has to toss in his cards and walk away. Can't fault those men for their actions if they were in over their heads."

Tom showed immediate concern. "You're a sight younger than either of those men, Judge. Aren't you afraid you'll be in over your head too?"

"I've come across a few snakes what needed their tails stomped on afore they was willing to sit still and listen up proper-like. I reckon they chose me for this here town because I don't scare as easy as some."

Tom showed his teeth again. "You sound like the kind of man we need, Judge."

"Gordy." Raylene's fingers dug into his arm hard enough that he about yelped from the sudden pain. "Help me down, so we can have a look inside our new home."

"Sure thing, ma . . ." He about called her *ma'am.* "Uh, mah sister," he finished quickly. Then he jumped down. The painful jolt between his shoulders reminded him that his injury still needed some time to heal. He hid the grimace and turned to help Raylene climb to the ground.

"I don't know why," Ellen Lawson said, scrutinizing him, "but I expected someone older. It must have been the way I interpreted the letter from the governor's office."

"Like I was telling your husband, ma'am,

age don't count much for experience," Joe replied to her observation. "I can tell you, I've done polished a good number of court benches with the seat of my britches these past few years."

"Open the door, Gordy," Raylene suggested, again tugging on his arm. "Let's go inside and have a look at our house."

Joe did as she asked, pulling open the door to allow some light into the building. He stepped through first and let his eyes adjust to the dimness. Raylene followed and stood beside him, not uttering a word.

The floor was hard-packed dirt, and the walls were wood planks with slivers of light showing through a few of the cracks. Several wooden benches lined either side of the room, and at the opposite end of the open space was a pulpit. It stood about four feet high and had a cross of polished wood attached to the face.

"The living quarters are to the rear," Tom said from behind them. "It isn't much, only one bedroom and a kitchen, but there's a pump out back for your water needs. You won't find better lodgings anywhere in town."

Raylene bit down on her lower lip. "But only one bedroom."

"We can park the wagon around to the

back." Joe was matter-of-fact. "I can sleep there nights till we add another room."

"If you need some help unpacking," Ellen offered, "Tom and I would be happy to stick around and lend a hand."

Raylene pivoted to face them. As if by magic, the radiant smile appeared again on her face. "I'm sure we can manage," she said. "We don't have all that many belongings."

Joe hadn't studied on it before, but when the notion came over her, Raylene could be about as cute as a kitten rolling in a bed of roses. And her smile was not only pleasant, but when her eyes shone brightly, her entire face radiated a luminous glow.

"We'll leave you to sort out your living quarters," Tom said. "However, we would be honored if you would join us for dinner tonight. You're probably tired from the long ride, and it might take you a little time to get organized for cooking and the like."

"That's very thoughtful of you," Raylene replied. "We'd be delighted."

"Our house is the one with the red brick chimney, behind the general store." Tom grinned. "You might have noticed the name, Lawson's Mercantile."

Raylene laughed politely. Joe didn't see anything particularly funny, but he did manage to muster up a somewhat dimwitted grin.

"Shall we say about six?" Ellen checked with Raylene.

"Yes, we'll be there."

Tom and Ellen said their good-byes and left the barn. The door barely closed behind them, when Raylene spun on Joe like a puma ready to pounce. So much for the charming posture she had displayed for the Lawsons. She appeared ready to claw his eyes out.

"What's the matter with you?" she demanded to know. "Where did you come up with such insipid adages?" She was practically foaming at the mouth. "Stomping on a snake's tail and polishing benches! Do you have any idea what they must think of you?"

"Dad-gum," Joe complained, "I only been a judge for two lousy minutes, and I'm already getting my branches trimmed. I was trying to be agreeable. I told you right off I wasn't cut out for this job."

"If you are unsure how to respond to a statement or question, just nod in agreement or let me answer."

"The man wasn't talking to you."

"Don't you see?" She altered her speaking, as if trying to make a child understand. "Your gambler-style witticisms and cowboy drawl will give you away in no time. We'll be invited to leave town before we even get settled."

"Look, lady" — Joe felt an increased warmth under the extra-snug collar, so buttoned to hide his bandage — "I didn't volunteer for this here chore. You done drafted me into it. I told you I'd do my best, and I'm a man of my word. But" — he transmitted a hard stare and used his superior height to combat the woman's ire — "I ain't going to stand for you to be digging in your spurs every time I open my mouth."

Raylene appeared ready to fire another barrage of heated words at him, but then she seemed to think better of it. She took a deliberate breath, deep enough that her bosom rose noticeably with the effort. After a long moment she exhaled the air and was once more completely civil.

"I'm sorry, Joe. I didn't mean to snap at you." She apologized with her words, but the embers of anger still burned in her eyes. "It's just that this obligation means a great deal to me. My father died while coming here to bring justice and order to the lives of these people. He was so very special, I feel morally obligated to complete his last assignment." Tears misted her eyes, reflective of her loss. "Can you understand what

I'm saying?"

Joe couldn't keep up his dander, not with the gal being so sincere and somewhat vulnerable. "Yes, ma'am," he said gently. "I understand."

"It's Raylene," she corrected.

Joe didn't have time to amend his address, because the door suddenly burst open, and two men entered the barn. Each wore a cocky sneer on his face and a gun slung low on his hip. It didn't take a second look to know they had come to start trouble.

CHAPTER THREE

"Good day to you, gentlemen." Raylene was immediately courteous and pleasant. "Is there something we can do for you?"

The first man leered at her and snickered. "I'm sure I can think of something you can do for me, honey."

Joe summed up the two newcomers at a glance. One fellow was slender, with bowed legs, big hands, and the long face of a hound dog. The man in front looked more the bullying sort, fairly stout, with sagging jowls and piggish eyes. Both men wore badges, and malice shone brightly in their faces.

The bullet-shaped brute sneered at Joe. "You the new judge?" He moved impudently over and planted his massive frame in front of him.

"If you've come looking to throw yourselves on the mercy of the court for past crimes, you're a little early," Joe told him with an easy manner. "You'll have to wait

60

until I have time to settle in and dig out my judging robe."

"We came to save your hide, Mister High-and-Mighty," the big fellow taunted. "I'm Bulldog Vern, and my pard here is Keno Roy." He paused to spit a stream of tobacco juice onto the floor and took a step closer, getting right into Joe's face. "We are deputies in this here town, and we shore don't need some shifty-eyed, twisted-thinking judge telling us how to handle our business. We come to help you pack your things."

"Better yet, to make sure you don't unpack," Keno joined in, moving to within a couple feet of Raylene. He allowed himself a rude gaze, covering her from toe-tips to bonnet. "Course, the lady here can stay."

Joe had dealt with enough pushy sorts to know when they were bluffing and when they were intent upon making trouble. Feigning a backward step, as if intimidated by Vern, Joe whipped out his gun and, in the same motion, clubbed the stout man smartly alongside his head. The force of the gun barrel striking him near the temple knocked him to his knees.

Before Keno could react, Joe had the gun cocked and aligned at his head. "Hold your hog leg!" he warned. "You so much as blink, and I'll send you to hell in a basket!"

61

Keno had started a grab for his gun but froze in midmotion, agape, staring down the muzzle of Joe's Peacemaker Colt. He slowly lifted his hands up even with his shoulders.

"Easy, Your Honor," he said, taking a step backward. "There wasn't supposed to be any gunplay."

Vern groaned and put a hand up to the welt on the side of his head. He managed to stagger to his feet but appeared dazed, as if he couldn't quite focus.

"You two boys, being deputies and all, should thank me for coming here. From now on, your only responsibility will be to catch the criminals. I'll deal out punishment. You might say we will be working as a team." Joe took a step back as he spoke, vigilant of keeping both men under his gun. "However, I don't want you coming into my courtroom thinking you can throw your weight around. Nor do I allow anyone to spit on the floor like your partner here. I take exception to things like that. You hear me, Keno?"

Keno bobbed his head up and down. "Yes, sir, Your Honor. I hear you loud and for shore."

"Now you apologize to the lady here for being disrespectful."

The tall man removed his hat and lowered his head. "I'm right sorry if I offended you, ma'am," he said solemnly. "I was only funning with you and shore do beg your pardon for being on the vulgar side."

"I accept your apology," Raylene said.

Joe waved the gun barrel, indicating to the unsteady brute. "Collect your pal and git."

Keno replaced his hat, put an arm around Vern's waist, then paused to give Joe a long look. "I got to admit, you won this round, Judge," he said, displaying something akin to admiration. "As for me, I'm damned impressed. I never met a judge like you before."

"You won't meet up with another judge like me again anytime soon," Joe agreed.

"A word of warning." Keno grew serious. "If you stick around Gold Butte and start enforcing real law, you'll likely be run out of town on a rail."

"A man who upholds the laws of the community can't be a coward, Keno. If you come back looking for trouble, I'll be here to accommodate you."

Instead of issuing a threat or a vow to get even, Keno grinned. "Judge, you shore 'nuff proved your point today. If trouble comes your way, you can count on me not be a part of it."

Joe did not reply, and Keno began to guide Vern toward the door.

"Did I get into a fight?" the big man asked groggily, staggering at his side, still disoriented and unsteady from the blow to his head.

"Weren't no fight, Vern. You was hit by a runaway freight wagon."

"Gotta watch where I'm going," Vern mumbled. "Didn't even see it coming."

"It come out of nowhere," Keno told him, "that's a fact."

Once the two men left the barn, Joe holstered his gun, expelled a breath of relief, and prepared himself for another tongue-lashing.

"I dare say you handled that situation very well," Raylene commented.

"Really?" he asked, not hiding his surprise.

She dismissed the subject and glanced around. "Let's have a look at our . . . living quarters. I'd like to unpack and clean up before we go to have dinner with the Lawsons."

Joe was taken aback by her calm demeanor. He had expected she would light into him like a starving cat after a crippled mouse. Instead, she set aside the confrontation with Vern and Keno as if it were unimportant. There was more to this gal than met the eye.

Relieved to put the incident aside, Joe led the way to the rear of the building. When they reached the door to the living quarters, he held it open for Raylene.

As the neighbors had described, two rooms had been built at the rear of the barn. They first checked the bedroom. It looked to have originally been sleeping quarters for the liveryman or hostler. The walls were covered with thick pasteboard and had been painted an off-yellow. There was a single dressing table and some hooks on one wall to hang clothing. The bed was a wooden frame with a mattress of straw covered with a thick canvas. Raylene took a moment to sit down on it and gave a nod of approval.

"This place has all the charm and refinement of a prison cell, but I suppose we can make do."

Joe played the gentleman and took her wrists to help her back up onto her feet. Then they turned their attention to the kitchen. Joe gave it a once-over and said, "Not much in the way of furniture, but I've stayed in a lot worse."

The small cubicle had a potbellied stove, two cupboards, and a work counter. The table was constructed of six-inch planks, but the top and edges had been sanded smooth. There were also two sturdy-looking stools. Raylene opened one of the cupboard doors. As she did so, a mouse scurried across the shelf and disappeared through a hole in the wall.

"It's like having our own house in the country," Raylene quipped. "We've even got a resident mouse."

"Once we get settled, maybe we can find us a cat."

Raylene rotated again and peered at him. Joe wondered what the strange look was for, until she asked, "How did you know to hit that man?"

"They came to start a fight," Joe replied with certainty.

"We had hardly even arrived. Why would they start a fight with you — a judge?"

"It was their way of drawing a line in the dirt and daring us to cross it," Joe replied. "You push a man the right way, he either has to fight or run. If the big fellow hadn't gotten a rise out of me with his bullying, Keno probably would have started to man-handle you. They wanted us to climb back into your wagon and set course for a more civilized town."

"You said you could read a man at a glance?"

"Yeah, most of them, ma'am."

"Raylene," she corrected.

Joe uttered a sigh. "This ain't never going to work. I don't know enough about the law to even fake being a judge."

"You just said you knew talking would do no good with those two deputies."

"That's the way I read the pair. I didn't figure to let them get the upper hand or maybe have you in tears."

She gazed at him, as if trying to read what he was thinking. "And that would bother you, seeing me in tears?"

"Yes, ma'am."

"Raylene," she again corrected. "You must learn to call me by my first name."

"It ain't proper."

"And stop using *ain't!*" Her voice rose an octave. "It makes you sound uneducated."

Joe arched his eyebrows. "I reckon that's 'cause I am uneducated."

His confession appeared to suddenly hit home. "Wait a minute!" she gasped. "You did attend school, didn't you?"

"Remember way back to yesterday," he queried, "when you trapped me into this here plan? You sure didn't hear me say anything about schooling whilst I was telling you the story of my life."

He thought the lady would burst the buttons on her bodice. Her face grew red, and she threw up her arms, clenched her hands into tightly balled fists, and uttered a muffled scream of frustration at the ceiling.

"My good Lord!" she lamented, whirling back at him like a dog about to attack. "Do you know how to read?"

"What difference does it make?" he teased. "I only have to listen to both sides of an argument, then make a decision on who is in the right. Won't need a lot of reading to do that job."

"How can you interpret a deposition if you can't read?" she demanded to know. "What about contract disputes or mining claim fraud? You have to be able to read!"

"You're the one who dragged me into this, ma'am." He continued to toy with her. "If you recall, I didn't raise my hand and volunteer."

"Gadfry!" she exclaimed. "I can't believe I didn't think about . . ." She didn't finish the sentence. Instead, she began to storm around the room, placing her hands on either side of her head, groaning as if she had a terrible headache. "What am I going to do? What can I do?"

"Don't get too riled up," Joe decided to interject after she had made three complete circles around the room. "Scholar done learnt me to read and write."

"Scholar?"

"You remember my telling you about him? He's the gambler who took me in for a time. He was a smart man."

She stared at him, wondering if he was making a joke or was serious. "Yes, I remember. And he taught you how to read and write?"

"I don't know every word there is, but I can usually figure out what something says." He grinned. "Besides, you'll be at my side. If I have trouble with some of the highfalutin lawyer lingo, I'll just bang the gavel and call for a temporary halt to whatever is going on. You can look over the writings and tell me what you think."

"It's called a recess." She fired the words at him hotly, angered that he had been teasing her. "And you can't always stop the proceedings. Sometimes you will have to make the decision without conferring with me."

"We can work out some sign language," he suggested. "You give me a nod or tap a finger, and I'll go along with your judgment. I figure I can bluff my way through the rest."

She stared at him as if he had swallowed about three forkfuls of locoweed. "These mine owners might have actual lawyers working for them. They will be familiar with the way a court operates and how a real judge behaves. You won't be able to fool them."

"I hate to waste a trump card on a deuce, but this was your idea, ma'am."

"Raylene!" She practically screamed her name. "How can I expect you to act the part of a judge, when you won't even call me by my first name?"

"All right, *Raylene.*" He bit off the name tightly, growing tired of the gal's continually finding a reason to be mad at him. "I told you I wasn't the best man you could have picked for this here job, but I gave you my word to try."

Raylene suddenly looked very tired. She walked into the next room, went to the bed, and sat down. "It seems hopeless," she muttered, completely demoralized. "My father's dream, his legacy, is over, finished. Even if I'm in court and we devise some signals, I don't see how we can make this work. I've failed him . . . failed him miserably."

Joe saw the tears well up in her eyes and hated his own ignorance. In a consoling gesture, he moved over and sat down at her side. After a moment he patted her on the shoulder.

"Listen to me . . . Raylene," he said gently. "You came up with this idea on your own, and I would be the first to admit, it has a number of holes in it, but I'm willing to pay my debt. Maybe I'll make a fool of myself and get us run out of town on a rail. I don't know. All I can say is, you seem to have your heart set on this, and I'll do my best to not let you down."

"You can't even stop using the word *ain't*," she pointed out.

"All right, so I . . . *amn't* so good at some things."

"There's no such word as *amn't*."

Joe frowned. "I figured that's what *ain't* means — am not."

"In essence, I suppose, but neither usage is proper grammar."

"Hoppin' horny toads, lady!" Joe complained. "You can't expect me to learn grammar and judging at the same time."

"I don't expect you to learn either one, Joe." Defeat was thick in Raylene's voice, and she looked ready to break down and cry. "It's over. It was a silly idea."

Joe jumped to his feet and glared down at her. "Ma'am, ever since I met you, you have shown more grit than most men would. You buried your father along the trail and took the bullet out of my back like a true pioneer. I know you've got a lot of smarts, and I've seen your courage and strength too. It don't

71

make no sense for you to bid this hand so high, then up and fold when the last chips are in the pot."

Her eyes were misty with tears, but she broke into a soft laugh. "Whatever was I thinking, Joe? From your manner of speech, there isn't any way we could ever hide the fact that you've been a gambler all your life."

"Why try to hide it?" Joe asked. "I never sat down and talked man to man with a real judge, but I'm betting most of them are just average guys with the same vices or faults as the rest of us. I don't have to pretend I never picked up a playing card. I'll bet a good many judges visit a casino or sit down for a game of poker. A judge has to do something with his free time."

"That's true," Raylene agreed. "Father enjoyed playing cards on occasion."

"There you are then," he said. "In my spare time, I like to play cards — nothing complicated about that. And you can give me one of them there law books to study so I can learn what the different terms mean."

"I do have a couple of father's law books. If you really think —"

"I think" — he cut off her skepticism — "we didn't come here for the fun of the ride. This is your plan, and you seem right capable to me, so I'm going to stick at this until you say quit."

A light suddenly beamed from Raylene's face, a radiance that emanated from within. Her eyes grew bright and full of life again. "Maybe you're right, Joe. We still might make this work!"

Keno walked into the sheriff's office, glanced at Pike Unger, and pulled around the chair opposite the desk. He straddled the chair like a horse and rested his forearms on the top of the backrest.

"How did it go?" Pike asked.

"Vern is over with the doc, getting looked at. He's seeing double since the judge clubbed him alongside the head with his pistol."

Pike's mouth dropped open, and he leaned forward in his chair and placed both hands on his desk. "What did you say?"

"You remember them last two old men who come here thinking they were going to be judges in Gold Butte?" Keno asked. "Well, this guy ain't in the same category, not by a long shot. He clouted Vern alongside the head and had me under his gun muzzle before either of us knew he was going to react."

"The new judge hit Bulldog?"

"Knocked a fair portion of the dust loose

in his rafters," Keno informed him. "I was about a whisker away from getting my head shot off too. I'm telling you, this new fellow ain't going to be as easy to deal with as those last two clowns. He's got some bark on his hide."

Pike's face twisted into an ugly mask. "What kind of judge pistol-whips a deputy?"

"In the judge's defense," Keno offered, "we did go over there to throw a scare into him. But instead of him getting the shakes and pleading for mercy, he turned the tables on us right sudden."

"He must be a tough old codger."

"Not all that old either," Keno replied. "I'd wager he ain't more'n thirty, maybe even a couple years younger than that."

Pike rubbed his hands together and sat back in his chair. "So he's a young buck, huh?" He snorted his contempt. "Probably drew this as his first assignment. The governor must have been right put out that his first two appointments were sent packing with their tails between their legs."

"I looked into Gordon Stanfield's eyes, Pike, and I can tell you this guy don't show fear. If he felt any, he sure hid it well."

"Let's not do anything more at the moment," Pike said. "First, I'll have a talk with Chase about the new judge. He can decide how to handle the situation."

"Not my place to say so, Pike, but it's his brother, Dunn, who owns most of Gold Butte. You think it's smart to always go by what Chase has to say?"

Pike waved a dismissive hand. "Dunn is too busy with his pretty wife and overseeing the saloon and business end of things. Chase is our man on the street, the one dealing directly with the miners and the company store. He pulls all the strings as far as keeping this town under our thumb. Dunn doesn't need to be bothered about the small stuff. He only cares that he can afford to dress up his lady like a queen and parade her about for all the world to admire."

"She's about as fine a woman as I ever set eyes on," Keno admitted. "I suspect if I owned Dunn's gold mine, I'd sure enough spend every cent I earned on her too."

"I always figured you for a soft head, Keno." Pike laughed. "Maybe I was aiming about a foot too high!"

Keno grinned. "It's no crime to have a heart, Pike."

"So long as it doesn't get you into trouble," he warned. "You go looking cross-eyed at Dunn's woman, and your life won't be worth shucks."

"Not me," Keno said quickly. "No way I would ever let the he-bull catch me looking too close at his woman. She's married to him, for one thing, and I like having my head right here on my shoulders for another. I'm not anxious to get it shot off."

"Yeah, you ain't *that* soft in the head *or* heart," Pike jeered. In a more serious vein he added, "I wouldn't say the same about Chase."

"I've seen him stare after Myra too," Keno said. "Man would be a complete fool to lust after his own brother's wife."

"Chase wants more than Myra. He wants everything Dunn has. Truth be told, I think he wants to *be* Dunn."

Keno decided they had gossiped enough. "I'll head back over to the doc's and pick up Vern. Doc'll probably suggest I put the big oaf to bed."

"If Bulldog isn't able, I'll need you for the night shift."

"I'll plan on it," Keno said. "Less noise sleeping here than over at the bunkhouse."

"You're a good man, Keno. I'll let Chase know about the new judge and see you back here about dark."

Tom and Ellen Lawson had two children, a boy of six and a girl, four. After a tasty meal of roast beef and baked potatoes, Ellen sent the kids off to play, while she and Raylene cleaned up the dishes. Tom, meanwhile, led Joe out back to a porch, where there were a couple of rocking chairs.

"We often sit out here in the evenings and watch the kids play until dark," Tom said. "Gold Butte has a lot of snow in the winter, but it can still be a very nice place to live."

They sat down in the rocking chairs, and Tom pulled out a cigar. "I usually have an after-dinner smoke. Would you care for one?"

"Never did care for the taste or smell of those things," Joe replied. "I tried a chaw of tobacco when I was younger, but spitting juice is sure enough a dirty habit."

Tom put a match to his smoke and took a short pull. "Everyone has to have a vice, I suppose."

"Yeah, mine is cards."

"No kidding?" Tom said. "You a gambling man?"

"I'll sit in at a friendly game," Joe told him. "Playing cards is relaxing for me."

"I've always tried to live a clean life," Tom mused. "I try to be a good father, good husband, and deal fairly with my customers."

"I reckon that's all anyone could ask of a

man," Joe told him. "Honest, hardworking, and taking care of your own — I'd call that being successful."

Tom took another puff on the cigar and turned to business. "As for you, Judge, this town is going to be a challenge. The smaller mine owners are controlled by the Estcott brothers. Dunn owns the biggest mine around, the company store, and one of the saloons. He also built the railroad spur for hauling ore to the smelter. Of course, it's his smelter too."

"And he's against having a judge in Gold Butte?"

"I don't believe it's the idea of a judge that worries him, it's the possible influence an honest lawman might have with the miners. Between the two Estcott brothers, they pretty much control the prices of everything here. Our goods have to be transported by their railroad, so they add additional shipping charges to the cost. Then Chase or the sheriff collects a twenty percent tax on everything we sell. It makes it impossible to keep the prices of our goods affordable."

"Dad-gum, twenty percent is a high tax."

"It started out at ten percent, and then Chase came around and doubled it a few months back. Many of the businesses are having a difficult time surviving."

"Sounds like Dunn Estcott has set himself up as a king."

"I'm not sure we can blame all of the problems on Dunn," Tom said. "I haven't heard any complaints about his railroad operation, the smelter, or even the saloon. But his brother and the sheriff have every other man jack in town under their heel, and I'm betting they don't want anyone coming in here and telling any of us that we have a right to a better way of life. Get out of line, and the sheriff will step in."

"I've been in a town or two like that before," Joe informed him.

"Part of our tax is to pay for our law enforcement and city improvements. I do offset that by being the town mayor, as the position allows me to deduct five percent of the store's earnings."

"So you still pay the house fifteen percent to stay in business," Joe said. "I've heard of dealers running gambling tables for less."

Tom took another pull on the cigar and continued to lay out the situation. "When you figure I try to operate on a twenty-five percent markup, yes, it is. Plus, I'm not allowed to carry anything the company store offers, such as miners' tools, work gloves, boots, explosives, or the like. It tends to limit how much we can sell."

"I begin to see some of the problems here in town."

"If someone tries to organize a protest, they end up with a busted head, courtesy of our law enforcement. If a miner mentions forming a union, he is escorted out of town and warned to never return."

"This just keeps sounding better and better," Joe said sarcastically.

"Estcott and the other mine owners don't want a union coming in here. It's another reason those owners are afraid of a real judge. A peaceful protest or threatened strike might actually be allowed to happen."

"How about you, Tom?" Joe changed the subject. "Can I count on your help with proceedings and support if I make some unpopular decisions?"

"I'm one hundred percent behind you, Judge."

"How about the other folks around town?"

Tom blew another cloud of smoke and watched it dissipate. "I believe you'll have more support than you might think."

"What about a courthouse? Do we have a building we use for that?"

"There is a claims office, but it's a single room above one of the saloons," Tom said, tapping a bit of ash into a small can next to the chair. Obviously, he was a careful smoker. "I was thinking we could convert your barn-sized room without much trouble," he went on. "It was already set up as a chapel. It has benches enough, so we only need to exchange the pulpit for a desk. If you wanted it to look more like a real courtroom, we could maybe build a platform for the desk and a witness chair."

"I suppose that will do," Joe said. Displaying a grin, he added, "I figure if I sentence the first few offenders to hang, there won't be as much need for a courthouse."

Tom laughed. "Judge, you're nothing like any other judge I ever met. Most of them are about as stiff as a post. You carry a gun and seem normal as sunshine."

"We all have to bend over to pull on our boots." Joe tried to be philosophical. "I figure life is like a hand of poker. Some men are lucky enough to get good cards and play the game to the end. Others have a bad draw or don't believe they have a winning hand and fold. A few stand back and watch, not willing to pay the ante or take any risks, so they never do play the game."

"Yes, sir." Tom continued to chuckle. "I'm sure looking forward to watching you deal out justice. It's going to be a blessing to have a town where my wife and kids can feel safe."

"Your wife seems like a very nice lady."

"She's a wonderful wife and mother — that's the truth."

"Tell me, Tom" — Joe changed directions — "how much trouble do you think this Dunn Estcott is willing to make for us?"

"I was afraid you might have already decided to leave town." Tom gave Joe a long look. "I saw Keno and Bulldog enter your building a few minutes after we had talked to you. I was trying to convince my wife to let me come back and help, when the two of them returned to the street. Bulldog looked as if he had walked into the working end of a hammer."

"They stopped by to say howdy and ask if we were going to stay," Joe said matter-of-factly. "I gave them our answer."

Tom chuckled, taking another pull on his cigar. "Yep," he said, displaying a grin, "you're not the ordinary cut for a judge, and that's the truth."

Joe didn't have to respond. Ellen and Raylene came out of the house to the back porch.

"I see you're smoking one of those horrible cigars again," Ellen said. "I really wish you would quit that nasty habit."

"Most every man has at least one vice," Joe said in Tom's defense. "Smoking a cigar is not as bad as most other vices. At least he's right here on the back porch and not up at one of the casinos, gambling away your money or sitting and drinking with a lady of dubious honor."

"Dubious honor?" Ellen laughed. "That's the first time I ever heard a dance hall girl described in such a way."

Joe caught Raylene's scowl and winked at her.

"We must be going," Raylene said, making an effort to hide her frown. "There's a lot we have to do."

Joe shook Tom's hand. "Thanks for the fine vittles and entertaining conversation."

"It's been our pleasure, Judge."

Raylene waved good-bye to the children and then led the way out of the house. She didn't speak to Joe until they were crossing the dark street.

"They seem very upstanding people."

"Yeah, and Tom offered his support on any decisions I might make."

Raylene cast a sharp look at him. "What kind of decisions?"

"The decisions that come with the job," Joe replied. "I figure, with him being mayor, it will add weight to any justice I deal out."

"That is good thinking on your part."

Joe felt relief. "Yeah?"

"According to Ellen, Dunn Estcott owns most of the town, but the real tyrant is his brother. He's the one who oversees the store and mines. He lays down the rules, and Dunn pretty much lets him do whatever he likes."

"I don't feel good about pointing my finger and telling people how to live their lives. After all, my own life has been about as poorly thought out as a man running barefoot through a cactus patch."

"You won't be setting down your own ideas of behavior, but making decisions based on the laws of the land."

They reached their new home, and Joe put out a hand to stop Raylene from entering. "Let me take a peek inside first," he said in a hushed voice, "just in case we have visitors."

Raylene stepped to one side, while Joe drew his gun and pushed open the door. He took a careful look around, but it appeared no one had come snooping while they were gone.

Joe went through and checked the living quarters, then stepped out back and made a quick sweep of the area around the wagon. He returned to the kitchen as Raylene was gathering up some of her traveling clothes.

"I need to do some washing tomorrow,"

she said. "If you have things to clean, I'll do them as well."

"That's mighty nice of you to offer, ma'am, but there's a laundry next to the saloon. I'll drop off my duds and let them do my cleaning."

Raylene wrinkled her brow. "That seems like a waste of money."

"Yeah, but it don't feel right for me to be putting my chores on you."

"I don't mind a little extra work."

"From looking at this place, we won't have a shortage of hard work," Joe replied. "Got to clean the courtroom from tip to top and make it more presentable."

"You mean the chapel?"

"Lawson told me this is about the only place in town big enough to use as a courthouse. If we have a trial, it will be held in the old chapel."

"I suppose that makes sense."

"Unless we want to tend to our business in the saloon." He grinned. "Reckon I'd feel a little more at home that way."

She made a face. "I prefer to use a renovated chapel instead."

"I'd best get a couple of locks for the front and back doors tomorrow. Wouldn't do to have anyone break into our courthouse."

"I'll allow you to use your own judgment

about the locks," Raylene said. Then, with a nervous glance around, she added, "You don't think anyone will bother us tonight, do you?"

Joe gave it some thought. "I'll block the back door and sleep in the courtroom for the night. If someone comes snooping around, they won't get past me."

"You're a very chivalrous man, Joe." Raylene's lips curled upward into a bit of a smile. "I'll feel much better with our both being under the same roof."

Joe about swallowed his tongue. "Think nothing of it, ma'am."

The smile vanished. "Joe." She sounded exasperated. "You have to learn to call me by my first name. If you use the *ma'am* word in front of anyone, they'll know we are not brother and sister."

"I keep trying, but it's like I told you before, I ain't never done any associating with a lady. It don't seem proper to be so familiar."

"We slept side by side on the trail and have been together for endless hours riding in my wagon. We are co-workers, two people on a mission to bring justice and order to this part of the country. We are partners in this endeavor."

"I was mostly recovering from a bullet

wound in your wagon, so that don't rightly count."

"Speaking of your injury, we should change the bandage."

"I took it off this afternoon, whilst you was getting ready for the meal with the Lawson family. It's pretty much healed up, except for being a mite tender."

"Are you sure?"

"Didn't even leave a drop of blood on the bandage." He smiled at her. "You're a pretty fair country doctor, ma'am." At her instant frown, he corrected his address. "I mean . . . Raylene."

Her expression softened, and she flashed a simper at him for his effort. The simple action caused him to suddenly feel good inside. It struck him how Raylene's smile had more charm than an ace-high flush.

"I'll throw my blankets onto the floor in the meeting room." He attempted to cover the sensation. "Tomorrow I'll get the locks in place and be able to bed down in the wagon."

"I'll sleep very well, knowing you are here to watch over me, Joe."

He felt the heat of embarrassment, so he quickly made his exit. The table would block the rear door, and he would sleep in front of the opposite entrance. The only way anyone would bother Raylene was over his dead body.

Conroy Masterson stormed about his office. Taller than most, his lanky frame had begun to bend with time. His shoulders were not as square and erect as they had been during his youth, but he was still a man who commanded respect. His searing gaze cowed the men of the posse, even the deputy marshal.

"You're telling me he got away?"

"The man was hit," the lawman said. "We saw him fold over the saddle, and we found blood on the trail. He must have crawled into a hole and died. Problem is, once he reached that rock mesa, we couldn't find hide nor hair of him."

"Then you don't know he's dead!" Masterson cried. "You can't be sure!"

The deputy twisted his hat in his hands. "No, sir, we can't be a hundred percent certain."

"I want to see his dead body or see him hanged!"

"Even if we had found him still alive, the US Marshal will be coming to town in a week or two. Once he looks into the gunfight, he and the judge are likely to rule it was self-defense. I figure we done the best we could to even the score."

Rather than argue, Conroy waved a hand to dismiss them. Once the men had shuffled out of the room, he walked to his desk. He should have known better than to send a bunch of amateurs to do a real man's job. Now, faced with the possibility of a judge overturning the warrant he had issued, it was time to act on his own. He knew of a special man for hire, a proficient and deadly bounty hunter. Though some considered him to be a back-shooting killer, he was competent and discreet.

Masterson pulled out a piece of paper and began to write.

CHAPTER FOUR

Joe woke early and set about constructing a temporary corral for their animals. He would need to fashion a lean-to and locate a regular watering trough. With three animals to tend, he also had to concern himself with arranging for feed. He could buy grain and grass hay from the livery, but it would be less expensive if he put the animals on a tether of some kind and moved them daily to a place where they could graze.

He had finished feeding and watering the trio of horses when the back door opened. Raylene stuck her head out and raised a hand to signal to him.

"Breakfast is ready!" she called.

Joe paused to rinse off his hands and entered the small kitchen area. There was an aroma of freshly cooked bacon, and he saw a plate of fried eggs. Raylene was at the stove, tending to flapjacks in a pan.

"Smells good," he said, sitting down on a

stool. "I didn't know we had eggs and bacon in the house."

"Ellen told me she would be at the store early, so I ran over and bought some things we needed. With the extent of the traveling Father and I had been doing lately, I haven't prepared a decent meal in weeks."

Joe told her about the livestock and how he would start building a fence for a corral. He also mentioned he would add the locks for the doors and see about getting enough lumber to partition off a section of the meeting room for a second bedroom.

"I feel as if I'm forcing you to do all the work," Raylene said.

Joe poured a bit of steaming hot syrup onto a flapjack. He took a bite and savored the delicious flavor. "For a meal like this, I would work dawn to dusk every day."

"Don't get used to it," Raylene cautioned. "Buying this food about broke me. I had no idea things would be so expensive."

"No farms around here for miles," Joe said. "They have to ship everything in by rail."

"All the same, we need to get a few cases, so you can start earning fees for consulting, settling disputes, and the like."

"I've got my own poke, ma'am," he replied, "enough to get us by for a spell."

Before she could reply to that, a tap came at the back door. Joe immediately reached for his gun, but the door opened a crack, and Ellen Lawson's head appeared.

"Hi!" she said cheerily, moving into the room. "I didn't want to barge in, but there's been a development you should be aware of."

"What kind of development?" Raylene asked.

"Victor Boggs was arrested late last night. He went home drunk and started to beat his wife." She sighed. "Victor has a boy and two girls. The boy is about ten, and the girls are both somewhat younger. Anyway, it was his son who ran to the jail to get help."

"So the guy is behind bars?" Joe queried.

"Keno was on duty and arrested him. I imagine the sheriff will be over to advise you of the facts in a short while."

"Thanks for letting us know," Raylene said. "We'll have to get the courtroom ready."

"I would stick around to help, but Tom is running the store, and I have to watch the kids."

"We'll be fine." Raylene had her magic smile back in place. "Soon as breakfast is over, we'll set up the benches and dig out the things we'll need from the luggage."

"Good luck!" Ellen said as she scooted back for home.

No sooner had the door shut than Raylene groaned. "This is all we need!" she lamented. "I haven't had time to work with you yet. How can we hold a hearing with you as green as the spring grass?"

"You told me a fair amount about the law and judging whilst we were making the trip here. I've a good memory." Joe offered a smile of encouragement. "You only have to explain some of the laws pertaining to this here type of violence, and I'll bluff my way through."

"This isn't a game of cards!" Raylene snapped. "What you demonstrate in handling your first case will define you to these people. I need time to work with you, to explain the letter of the law and how to manage and dispense justice in the courtroom. I can't tell you how to handle a case in a matter of —"

"Hallo, the house!" came a gruff voice from the main door.

Joe pushed his plate aside and walked in to see a rather large man with a sagging paunch on the far side of the room.

"I'm Sheriff Pike Unger," he said importantly. "I'm looking for Judge Gordon Stanfield."

"Now you're looking *at* him, Sheriff," Joe answered, walking over to meet him.

Pike was probably in his thirties, an inch taller than Joe, and quite a bit heavier. He wore an expensive Stetson and a fancy, be-spangled vest over a cotton red-and-black print shirt. His boots were expensive and polished to a high sheen, while a heavy Navy Colt hung low on his hip.

"Younger than I expected," Pike said, "although Keno told me you were not near as old as the last two judges who come to town."

"It was decided my youth and energy might come in handy here," Joe lied. "What can I do for you, Sheriff?"

Pike explained about Victor Boggs's being arrested, then shrugged. "If you ask me, some women have to be put in their place on occasion. Something like this, we usually hand out a fine and turn the guy loose." With a smirk, he added, "But with you be-ing the new justice of the peace in town and looking to make a name for yourself, I figured I would let you handle the matter."

"I'm obliged at your being so thoughtful and forthright, Sheriff. I'd be glad to listen to the case. Does the gent have himself a lawyer to stand up with him, or is he going to go it alone?"

"Being that Boggs is a miner, Chase Estcott — he oversees the mine and the company store — is going to let the Estcott lawyer handle the defense."

"How about a prosecutor?"

"Never used one before," the sheriff admitted, the smirk still playing on his lips. "We always used a tribunal approach and did our own asking of questions. I've heard a defense lawyer can be anyone who wants to stand up with the accused. Don't know all that much about the prosecuting side."

"Fair enough," Joe said. "When did you have in mind for this trial to take place?"

"How about ten this morning?"

"Fine," Joe told him. "I'll expect you and the prisoner at ten."

Pike only partially hid his snicker and turned around. He attempted to stride from the room with a swagger, but his potbelly caused him to waddle like a duck who had dipped his bill into a bucket of tainted whiskey a few too many times.

The door barely closed before Raylene pounced on him.

"Joe, for Heaven's sake!" she wailed. "Ten o'clock? We have less than two hours to prepare you for your first case!"

"How tough can it be?" he asked.

"How tough?" She fairly hissed the words.

"It's a domestic dispute! Do you have any idea how hard it is to handle a case like this and not alienate everyone in town?"

"I've got you to coach me," he pointed out.

"It's a no-win situation, Joe. The wife can't testify against her husband, as that's against the law. The kids won't get on the stand because they are too young. You have no witnesses to an actual beating taking place, and — you heard the sheriff just now — a good many men believe it is the right of a man to discipline a wife from time to time."

"The hell you say!"

She continued to glare at him. "Yes, I do say! And worst of all, there is no proper verdict. If you put the man in jail, he loses his job, and his family starves. If you give him a warning and let him go, he'll beat her again tomorrow or the next day. Don't you understand? It's a case you can't win. You'll look bad no matter what you do."

Joe finally raised a hand to silence her objections. "All right, ma'am, we knew they were going to toss a couple jokers at us on the first deal. That's fine. We've got a few cards we can play too." She started to protest, but he shook his head to stop her. "No time for debate," he told her frankly.

96

"What I need to know are the legal words or terms I might need, so I can sound like a judge."

"I can't teach you that in less than two hours!"

"I told you I'm a quick learner. You trot me through how a judge behaves and quote me the laws and technical stuff I need to know. We can set up the courtroom while we talk."

"But, Joe, this isn't going to —"

"It's the cards we were dealt, ma'am," he cut her off sternly. "Rule One: if you can't afford the ante, you don't sit in at the game. These courthouse rules might use different terms and all, but I figure practicing law is no different than playing poker. There are ways to win, even if you have been dealt a bad hand. We'll show these people we're here to stay."

Raylene uttered another groan. "I suppose you're right about our having no choice. Let's hope only a few people show up."

"I'm going to finish breakfast, and then we can get to work."

"A last meal for the condemned used to be reserved for the prisoner," she quipped. "Why do I feel it will be our last meal instead?"

■ ■ ■ ■

Dunn Estcott stood at the front window of his house. He could see a few people beginning to make their way over to the provisional courthouse. After hearing how the new judge had handled the two men his brother sent to run him out of town, he was mildly curious.

"Did I hear right, Dunn?" Myra asked from behind him. "Is there going to be an actual trial today?"

"Not a real trial, honey," he replied. "It will be little more than a hearing and the dispensing of a fine. Victor Boggs was drinking and lost his money in the casino again last night. Like the good loser he is, he went home and took it out on his wife and kids."

"He doesn't seem the type," Myra said. "I spoke to him and Mary at the last social dance we had, and Mr. Boggs seemed very polite."

"Give him a few drinks and take his money," Dunn said dryly, "and you'll see a different side of him."

"Are we going to attend?" There was a hopeful note in her voice. "I've got several pretty gowns that I've never had a chance to wear. It seems like ages since I was able to dress up special."

Dunn frowned. "It's only going to be a dull hearing, my love. I doubt it will last more than ten minutes."

"It would give us a chance to greet the new judge and his sister." Myra continued her quest. "Ellen had them over for dinner last night."

"When did you see Ellen?"

"I went down to the store this morning for some coffee beans. The coffee in the cupboard had some kind of tiny bugs crawling in it."

"I don't know of many insects that eat coffee beans," Dunn said.

A frown line creased Myra's brow. "I don't care if they were resident diners or uninvited trespassers, Dunn. I'm not going to have a cup of coffee and wonder what the little buggers were doing on my coffee beans!"

Dunn recognized the look in Myra's eye. Her dander was beginning to rise, and it wasn't just about coffee. He knew, if he didn't take her to watch the court proceedings, she would sulk around the house and not talk to him. He would be miserable for a week. Rather than argue or suffer her wrath, he decided the smart move was to agree without protest.

"I think you're right, Myra."

"About the coffee?"

"Not the coffee, honey," he said, displaying an easy grin. "I think we should attend the hearing. I'd like to see how you look in that yellow dress with the white lace, the one we bought on our last trip to Denver."

"Oh, yes! Yes!" she burst out graciously. "I've been dying to find a reason to wear it."

His hunch paid dividends at once, for she sprang over and hugged him tightly. "Thank you, Dunn!" she exclaimed, leaning back to flash him a bright smile. "I'll be ready in fifteen minutes!"

He watched her mince out of the room, and his misgivings about going to the courthouse were put to rest. Beyond that, he felt a surge of gratification. Nothing lifted his spirits more than when he could make Myra happy.

He went to his closet and chose one of his best jackets to wear. Myra loved to be the center of attention, while he was both content and proud to be her escort. It hadn't been easy, keeping up with a girl ten years younger than himself. Dunn had chosen Myra for his bride because of her youthful beauty and poise. She, in turn, had been seeking a man with position, wealth, and security. It was a fair exchange, each of them using what they had to in order to get what they wanted in return.

His one regret was the fact there were no children. Myra had been unable to conceive. If he had been dogmatic about kids, it might have torn their marriage apart, but, instead, their mutual disappointment had made them more dependent upon each other.

His brother, Chase, arrived a few minutes later with Bulldog Vern at his side. Chase knew to leave Vern in the hall and entered the room alone.

"What's on your mind, little brother?" Dunn asked, once Chase had closed the door.

"I'm going to have Lavar defend Boggs," he said.

"Why should Lavar defend Boggs?"

Chase laughed. "To make the judge look like a fool. Lavar will eat him alive."

"I suppose it could make the case a little more interesting."

"I was thinking maybe me and a couple of the boys ought to be there too — stir the place up a bit."

"Why should you do that?"

"The tough-guy judge told Keno he would allow no nonsense or spitting in his courtroom. I thought we might test his mettle."

"I assumed you had such an idea in mind

when you sent Keno and Vern calling on the judge yesterday," Dunn said. "That was a stupid move."

"You didn't have no complaint about my running the other two judges out of town."

"The question is why, Chase? Where's the harm in allowing a genuine judge to handle any crimes or litigation cases? We're on solid ground. I've got a proper deed or title to everything I own, and we aren't breaking any laws."

"You might be protected, big brother," Chase complained, "but I'm out there on the front lines, taking a lot of heat. I deal with the miners and have to keep them in line. I do the hard business of controlling the credit at the store and making sure everyone is paying his taxes in town. I'm the bad guy here, not you."

"I can't oversee the railroad, smelter, the saloon, the mine, and the company store by myself," Dunn reminded him. "It's why we agreed to split this up from the very beginning."

"You decided how to divide the duties," Chase corrected. "I'm all right with that, but now the people around town are flocking to meet the new judge like ants to a honey spill. I don't like the idea of allowing someone in here who might end up siding against us. We should do something before the man gets his feet firmly planted and we can't move him."

"There will be no move to disrupt the trial today, Chase."

"Bulldog wants to get even with the judge for getting clubbed!" his brother cried. "You expect us to let that guy get away with what he did?"

Dunn waved a dismissive hand. "Vern has been a bully all his life. I'd say he got what he deserved. Besides, it's enough the new judge will have to deal with Lavar. He has fifteen years experience and has worked some very big cases."

"It's the wrong move!" Chase snapped, livid with his brother. "Even if Lavar shows the judge up, the people might get the idea he's for real. If that gavel-banger manages to plant some seeds, we'll be forced to pull roots later. We ought to act now, before he gets himself a bunch of supporters."

"Myra wants to meet him." Dunn told him the truth. "I'll watch how the hearing plays out and see if the guy presents any real threat to us and the other mine owners."

" 'Myra wants'!" Chase snorted his disgust. "It's always what Myra wants! I swear, you ain't got the backbone of a slug since

103

you married her, Dunn."

Dunn bore into his brother with a cold, level gaze. "Don't forget who is the top dog around here, Chase. I'm the one who brought you in to help run things, and I'm the one who makes the decisions."

"Yeah, you're the boss," Chase admitted, but the words were thick with contempt. "But you gave me reign to oversee collecting the taxes, the store, and the mine. I see a lot more unrest than you do at the saloon or running the railroad operation."

"I'm aware of how hard you work, Chase, and I appreciate it." Dunn let the matter drop. "Today, you and the boys can relax. I'll watch the judge in action and maybe have a few words with him after to get a feel for what he's all about."

"I still say it's a mistake to let him have free roam, Dunn."

"It's my decision, little brother," Dunn said firmly. "If you don't like the way I run things, maybe you ought to think about getting yourself a real job."

Chase backed down from his hostile posture. "I'm only thinking we shouldn't take any chances, Dunn. I'd hate to think you were going soft because of your wife."

"Leave Myra out of this," Dunn warned.

A thin smile played upon his brother's

lips. "Sure thing, Dunn, whatever you say goes. I know that."

Dunn did not pursue Chase's insolence. It seemed the man had grown more obstinate and troublesome every day since he had wed Myra. His younger brother was like a buck testing his horns against the aged leader of the herd. But there were other factors involved. Chase truly resented Myra. To his way of thinking, she had come between them . . . and she had. Once wed to the youthful beauty, Dunn had taken on a new maturity and was now willing to reason things out. Before he met his wife, he would have turned Chase loose to do whatever he wanted. Unfortunately, his brother had not made the adjustment to his more mellow lifestyle. He was confounded about why Dunn had suddenly changed. He didn't know love made a man more mindful of his actions. Dunn wanted Myra to be proud of him; he needed her respect, and that was something Chase didn't understand.

"One thing you have to admit is pretty strange," Chase commented, when Dunn did not offer another word. "Keno said the judge got his gun into play awfully quick for a guy who sits on a bench and spouts law and justice."

"Yes, a judge with the speed of a gunman," Dunn surmised. "It makes sense to send such a man here, especially after the way you frightened off the other two."

"Well, if you change your mind and decide to get rid of him, you only have to say the word," Chase vowed. "Me and the boys will sure enough run him off, even if we have to drag him behind a horse and burn his makeshift courthouse to the ground."

"I don't want to do anything that might instigate an uprising by indignant miners and the other businessmen in town, little brother. It's exactly what we're trying to avoid."

"Have it your way," Chase said with a shrug. "You say to sit on our hands, we sit on our hands."

Dunn hid his impatience. "I'll see you later."

Chase didn't argue further but turned around and headed back to join Vern. Dunn watched him go, concerned at his brother's growing impertinence. One day, perhaps very soon, Chase would tire of riding in the back of the wagon and challenge him for the reins.

Dunn adjusted his jacket and checked his reflection in a mirror. When he turned around, he discovered that Myra was ready to go to the hearing. She was as flawless as an exquisite, finely crafted doll. Dunn blatantly admired her, and she glowed under his scrutiny. She was everything he could have ever wanted in a wife — beauty, refinement, and charm. He would not risk destroying what they had together, even if it meant sending his brother packing.

From behind the kitchen door, Raylene peeked out for the hundredth time. When she looked over at Joe, she wore a worried frown.

"I didn't know there were so many people in all of Gold Butte," she lamented. "Everyone in town must be out there. Most of the benches are full, and they're standing three-deep against the walls and packed right out the door!"

"It's a showdown," Joe replied. "All the cards have been dealt. It's time to spread out your hand for all to see."

"I think I'd rather fold," Raylene said weakly.

"Not on your life!" Joe scolded her for her display of defeat. "Give the signal to Tom, and put on your poker face. It's time to play this here game."

Tom had closed his store for the hearing and accepted the position of court bailiff.

He was watching for Raylene to give him the nod. When she did, he stepped out in front of the pulpit.

"Quiet down, folks," he said over the din in the room. "I wish to make an announcement before we get started."

The room fell silent, and he continued. "The judge hasn't had time to unpack properly, let alone convert this old chapel into a proper courtroom. Therefore, he will preside from the pulpit, and the witnesses will use the chair we've placed next to it. The front row is for the prosecution and defense, along with the sheriff and defendant."

He paused and looked out over the room. Then he gave his prepared speech. "Hear ye, hear ye, the court will now come to order. All rise for the Honorable Gordon Stanfield!"

Joe trod on the hem of the long robe with his first step and stumbled. Fortunately, he was not yet in sight of the audience. He quickly hiked the robe up a couple inches so he wouldn't trip during the remainder of the walk. Sucking in a swallow of courage, he strode to the pulpit. Raylene entered next and walked past him to take her place on the front bench.

"Be seated," Joe told the crowd, then

added quickly, "those who have a place to sit."

Taking a second deep breath, he looked over the spectators. Raylene was right about the crowd; it appeared everyone in town had shown up.

"What is the first order of business?" Joe asked, remembering Raylene's instructions.

Tom looked at a piece of paper in his hand and read it aloud. "The city of Gold Butte versus Victor Boggs — one count of assault and battery."

Joe gave Tom a nod of thanks and waited until he moved off to stand against a wall, there being no remaining seats left. He gazed over at the accused, presently clean-shaven, a modest-looking man of about forty, clad in his Sunday-go-to-meeting clothes. The guy did not look like the violent type, but his wife — seated in back of him — had a dark swelling under her left eye.

"Mr. Boggs," Joe said to the man, "how do you plead?"

"For the defense." A smooth-haired jackal seated next to Boggs sounded off and rose to his feet. Fancy duds, a string tie, with a smile like he had just drawn four aces, this was the Estcotts' lawyer. "Lavar Crump," he introduced himself. "I am representing

Mr. Boggs for this hearing. He pleads not guilty."

Joe immediately disliked the man's arrogance but continued. "Very well, Mr. Crump," he said. "But I warn you, any stunts to lighten the brutality of Mr. Boggs's actions will not be tolerated. If your client wishes to be a man and fess up to what he did, he should make that statement now."

Boggs blinked in surprise, and Lavar sputtered. "Your Honor! You can't . . ."

Joe whipped out his gun and set it down hard on the pulpit. The action silenced the lawyer at once.

"In my court, everyone is allowed to have his say." Joe directed his attention at Boggs. "You want to have a lawyer, that's fine. But I believe in justice, Mr. Boggs. The harder I have to work to get justice, the less lenient I'm going to feel. I want that understood."

Boggs glanced at the lawyer. Lavar gave him a sharp look, and he cowered at once. "This here is my lawyer," he muttered. "I'll leave it in his hands."

"As it seems this town doesn't have an actual prosecutor, I'll appoint one." Joe went forward with the proceedings. "Miss Raylene Stanfield has studied law longer than I have myself, so I reckon she's the best person for the job. Unless anyone has objections, Miss Stanfield is going to handle the prosecution."

Raylene's lower jaw about hit the floor. She stared at Joe as if he was making some kind of fantastic joke. When he remained standing at the pulpit, waiting, she managed to regroup a measure of her composure and stand up.

"Your Honor, I am ill-equipped to handle this case. I know practically nothing about the circumstances."

"Feel free to speak to anyone you like, and do the best you can." Joe again pushed ahead. "Mr. Crump, I'll let you lead off. Do you have anything to say on behalf of the defense?"

Lavar stepped up and displayed a professional smile. "As I'm sure Your Honor is aware, a woman cannot take the stand against her husband. As for this man's offspring, children are easily manipulated and have consistently proven to be poor witnesses in a court of law. It is our contention that Mrs. Boggs walked into a door — an unfortunate accident, but an accident nonetheless. I respectfully request that the charges against my client be dismissed."

Joe averted his attention to Raylene. "What does the prosecution have to say about this?"

"If it pleases the court" — Raylene was succinct and clear with her delivery — "we do have testimony that can be given here today."

"Proceed."

"Mr. Keno Roy, would you take the stand?" she directed.

Tom was quick to swear in the witness, and Raylene asked Keno to describe the events leading up the arrest of Victor Boggs.

"His boy come to the jail last night . . . must have been near midnight. He was frightened and crying."

"Did he say why?"

"Said his pa had hit his ma."

"Objection!" Lavar stated emphatically. "It is the hearsay of a child."

Joe looked at Raylene for help, and she quickly responded. "We are not declaring the hearsay statements to be factual, Your Honor. Mr. Roy is simply attesting to the events leading up to the arrest of Mr. Boggs."

"I rule for Miss Stanfield on this one, Crump," Joe said. "Go ahead."

Raylene looked a little piqued, but she remained poised. "Continue with your testimony please, Mr. Roy."

"I went straight to the Boggs' house and found Mrs. Boggs sitting on the floor in the main room. She was bleeding from the nose and had a swelling under one eye."

"Did she tell you what happened to her?"

"No, ma'am."

"What happened next?"

"Vic smelled of liquor and come at me, fixing to toss me out of his house. We wrassled about some, and I got him in an arm-lock. He come along real easy after that."

"Have you been called to the Boggs' place of residence before?"

"One other time, but it turned out to be mostly yelling going on. This is the first time he done hit his wife."

"Objection!" Lavar howled like a stepped-on pup. "He is making a claim of what happened, Judge. He can't put that into the record as fact."

Joe caught the wink of Raylene's left eye. He couldn't remember what that meant, so he waded through on his own. "Your point is well taken, Crump. We'll ignore that last statement." He was relieved to see that Raylene was pleased with his answer, and he continued. "Any further questions for Keno here?"

"No, Your Honor," Raylene replied. She rotated to look at Crump and said, "Your witness."

"Mr. Roy" — Lavar's tone was smug — "did you witness my client striking his wife?"

"No."

"Has Mrs. Boggs ever come forward to ask for the law's shelter or protection?"

"No."

Lavar shook his head as if unable to understand why he was even talking to Keno. "As far as you know, isn't it possible that Mrs. Boggs could have ran into a door and injured herself?"

Keno grinned. "Yeah, and it might have been a garden rake or someone throwing rocks, but it sure ain't likely."

Lavar whirled on Joe. "Your Honor, this witness is making a clandestine accusation with his remark!"

Joe pondered the word *clandestine* and had no idea what it meant. He glanced at Raylene, and she again blinked her left eye.

"Your point is well taken, Mr. Crump. Please continue."

"I have no more questions for this witness."

Raylene conferred with Ellen while Joe dismissed Keno from the witness stand. He gave her a moment to finish whispering back and forth before putting his attention on her.

"Do you have any more witnesses, Miss Stanfield?"

"Yes, Your Honor," she said. "The prosecution calls Dunn Estcott to the stand."

That announcement raised eyebrows and clearly shocked many of those present. Most everyone in the audience mumbled or whispered to his or her neighbor.

Dunn appeared stunned but rose to his feet. He was a handsome sort, past his early prime but still fit and athletic in build. He wore a nice suit and had been sitting with the prettiest woman Joe had ever set eyes on.

Tom seemed a little nervous about swearing in the king of Gold Butte, but he got the job done.

"Mr. Estcott," Raylene began, "as you own the casino, I assume you are aware of most of what transpires there. Is that true?"

"I like to be kept informed," he admitted.

"Are you familiar with Mr. Boggs?"

"He is a frequent customer."

"Have you or your men ever had to remove him from the saloon physically?"

Dunn cleared his throat. "On occasion."

"Would that be for drinking to excess and becoming violent?"

"I object!" Lavar shouted, standing up. "What is the relevance of this line of questioning?"

Raylene was equally quick. "To show cause and effect, Your Honor."

"Sounds like a fair question," Joe told Lavar. Then he looked at Dunn. "You can answer, Mr. Estcott."

"The answer is yes. Victor does sometimes drink to excess and has become rowdy in the past."

"What about his gambling?"

"Mr. Boggs often gambles at the casino. To my limited knowledge I believe he loses more than he wins."

"And he has previously started fights in your establishment?" Raylene asked.

"As I stated before, he has been removed on more than one occasion."

"Thank you, Mr. Estcott," Raylene said. "No more questions."

Joe hid the smile he felt as he looked over at the perplexed lawyer. "Do you wish to ask any questions of this witness?"

Lavar stared at Dunn, as if trying to decide what Dunn wanted him to do. Dunn, however, maintained a calm outward demeanor and offered not the slightest help.

"Uh, I have no questions for this witness."

Dunn was dismissed, and Joe asked Raylene, "Do you have any other witnesses to call?"

"The prosecution rests," she said professionally.

"What about you, Lawyer Crump?" Joe inquired. "Do you have anyone else to testify on behalf of your client?"

"There has been nothing proven concerning the complaint that is before the court," Lavar stated emphatically. "The testimony of the witnesses for the prosecution have produced nothing more than hearsay and speculation."

Joe glanced at Raylene. She had her hands folded in her lap, but two fingers were showing. That was the signal to give Boggs a small fine.

"A court verdict should not be about who has the most able lawyer or who has the most money and power," Joe began. "Neither should it be about a guilty person's escaping punishment through trickery and deceit. There should only be one rule in a courtroom: the innocent go free, and the guilty are punished."

Joe pointed a finger at the defendant. "Stand up, Victor Boggs!"

The man rose to his feet, hands locked together below the waist, both head and eyes lowered, awaiting the verdict.

"I would like to believe that, when you are sober, you are a decent and honest man,

117

Mr. Boggs. I wonder if you would mind turning around for a moment." Joe's voice grew cold. "I want you to take a good look at the mother of your children."

Victor glanced up at Joe in mystification, then rotated slowly to face his wife.

"A rather handsome woman, if you ignore the black eye, isn't she, Mr. Boggs?"

"I object to this outlandish display!" Lavar shouted. "It is a humiliation to my client."

"Your objection is noted," Joe told him without emotion.

"Mr. Boggs" — Joe went on with his own experiment — "what would you do if another man had done this to your wife? Would you simply shrug it off or forget about it? If some other drunk punched your wife in the face, would you lie to your kids and friends and neighbors and tell them she had walked into a door?"

Victor's shoulders sagged with his shame.

"Mr. Boggs, do you honestly believe there is any reason in the world for a man to hit his wife, other than for possibly catching her cheating with another man?"

"Your Honor," Lavar objected again, "this sort of harassment is without precedent."

Joe glowered at the lawyer. "Save your speechifying until your closing, Mr. Crump, or I'll hold you in contempt."

Lavar paled noticeably and sat down.

"Mr. Boggs" — Joe returned to the case at hand — "I ask you again, before this court, in the presence of your wife and all those here who know you are guilty — how do you plead?"

Victor slowly pivoted back around to face Joe. Tears flooded his eyes and left tiny trails down both cheeks.

"I done it," he said hoarsely. "I'm ashamed to admit it — warn't the first time neither. I told my wife I was sorry — damned sorry! But I sure enough hit her last night."

Joe looked over at Raylene. "Does the prosecution have anything to say?"

"We ask only for a suitable punishment, Your Honor."

"Council for the defense?" Joe asked Lavar.

The lawyer shook his head. "You eliminated my closing argument by coercing a guilty plea from my client. We await your decision and ask that the court show mercy for this man's temporary loss of self-control."

Joe didn't hesitate. "The court accepts your guilty plea, Victor Boggs. Do you have anything to say before I pronounce sentence?"

Boggs continued to blink back tears as he turned his head from side to side. "I regret hitting my wife. That's all I have to say."

Joe again saw Raylene displaying two fingers, but he didn't care for the punishment. Instead, he gave Boggs a long look.

"I sentence you to ninety days," Joe said.

There was an immediate shock and grumbling throughout the large gathering. A sea of angry faces appeared, and Joe wondered if some of the townfolk were going to attack the podium. Such a long sentence meant the likely loss of the man's job and his being able to support his family.

"The conditions" — he spoke loudly, so as to stop the mutterings — "are these, Victor Boggs." He picked up his pistol and tapped the handle butt on the podium to control the noise of the crowd. Once everyone had grown quiet, he continued.

"You are not allowed to set foot inside a saloon or casino for ninety days," he instructed. "You also will not gamble or bet on anything with anyone for ninety days. Most important, you will not strike your wife or children again without first asking my personal permission." He let the words sink in. "You will also turn your weekly pay over to this court every single week for those ninety days. The court hereby appoints

Raylene Stanfield to work with Mrs. Boggs to oversee the spending of your money for those ninety days."

The angry faces all magically turned to wonder and puzzlement at Joe's decree. He decided that was an improvement and went on.

"Lastly, I don't want to ever see you standing before this court again for mistreating your wife or children. If that happens, I'll have the prison wagon parked by the door, and you will end up busting rocks at a penitentiary until you rot."

Boggs was dumbfounded. His eyes were wide and his mouth agape.

"Do you agree to the terms of this here deal, Mr. Boggs?"

Still stunned, he began to bob his head up and down.

"Just remember this, Mr. Boggs. If you disobey any one of these conditions, you will be charged with contempt of court and shipped off to prison. The original sentence of ninety days will be served and an additional ninety days added to your time. Do you understand?"

"Uh, yeah," Boggs answered.

"Yeah, what?" Joe prompted him.

"I mean, yes, Your Honor," he replied a second time, but in a loud and clear voice.

"This court is adjourned," Joe announced. With a swish of his robe, he whirled about and left the room, closing the door behind him.

"Son of a gun!" Tom exclaimed, displaying a wide grin. "That wily son of a gun!"

CHAPTER FIVE

Raylene was surrounded by a mob of people before she had a chance to escape. Ellen gave her a hug, and several others patted her on the back, saying what a good job she had done. It was a first for her, being the center of attention and having won her first case.

The people continued to mill about for some time, and finally Joe returned, minus the long black robe, outwardly as nonchalant as if this had been an everyday ordeal.

A good many of those remaining lined up to speak to him. Raylene managed to make her way to his side, and they worked their way around the room until they were at the exit. This way, they could funnel the people out of the court and still speak to each one.

Most of those passing by paused to shake Joe's hand or say a word of welcome. However, the line stopped when Dunn and his wife reached the door.

"We weren't exactly introduced," the man said, regarding Joe with an astute scrutiny. "Of course you know I'm Dunn Estcott. I own the Silver Lady Mine and a few other things around town. This is my wife, Myra, and we would like to welcome you to Gold Butte, Judge Stanfield."

"Thanks for coming," Joe said, meeting the man's candid stare with a cool appraisal. "You were a real help with the trial."

Dunn chuckled. "Very shrewd of your sister to put me on the stand. It did give my lawyer pause as to how to proceed."

"My sister knows the law better than I do," Joe said truthfully, the comment bringing a smile to Dunn's face, "and we certainly appreciate the welcome."

"First time I ever met a judge who brandished a Colt Peacemaker during a hearing."

Joe read the glint of a challenge in the man's eyes, but he chose to ignore it.

"Holding a public hearing doesn't mean people are all going to behave, Mr. Estcott. I wasn't sure of the reception we would get."

"This was a very exciting hearing." Myra spoke up, smiling. "When it started, I was sure Mr. Crump would get Mr. Boggs off without censure, and I didn't feel that was right. You have a most unique way of dealing out justice. I thought the punishment quite appropriate."

"I hope he can turn things around in the next ninety days. He has a nice-looking family, and it would be a shame to lose them because of his weakness for gambling and drinking."

The lady beamed another of her dazzling smiles. "Well, I think you made a good impression all around."

Joe smiled at her. "Always tough holding court the first time in a new town, ma'am. I felt about as uneasy as a cat trapped in a pen of hounds, standing behind that pulpit."

Myra laughed politely and gave Dunn a nudge to get him moving. They were a nice-looking couple, though Dunn appeared half-again the young woman's age. Joe didn't have time to look after them, as the line of exiting people continued.

One gent, who seemed to have come to the hearing alone, passed Joe by but stopped to take hold of Raylene's hand. "It's a real pleasure having you here in Gold Butte, dear lady," he said. "I'm Steven Brock. I write and publish the weekly Gold Butte newsletter and am also the town sign painter." He flashed two rows of sparkling white teeth at her. "The cross on the meeting house was gratis from back when the building was donated to become a church."

"Raylene Stanfield," Raylene replied, rewarding him with one of her fabulous smiles. "I'm pleased to meet you."

"I would very much like to interview you for the newsletter," Steve told her. "Perhaps we could get together this afternoon or tomorrow?"

"Interview me?"

"Yes, dear lady," Brock said, practically drooling. "For a commentary on the first practicing female lawyer in Colorado. The story might be picked up by the larger newspapers in Denver or even back east. It is a groundbreaking achievement."

"I'd like that," Raylene replied sweetly. "Let's make it tomorrow."

Brock's eyes lit up like those of a man who had just drawn his first royal flush. "If you would allow me, I'd be honored to do the interview over lunch."

The offer caused Raylene to hesitate. "Lunch?"

"The hotel has an eatery. It's nothing ostentatious, but their food is quite tasty."

"It sounds inviting."

The man lifted a hand, as if he was going to swear on the Bible. "I am a strictly honorable man, dear lady, and it would be my extreme pleasure."

Raylene flicked a minute glance at Joe. He was busy shaking hands with a miner and concealed his intense interest in her response. When she said, "Very well," he clenched his teeth together hard enough to crack a molar.

"It's a date then," Brock told her gleefully. "I'll collect you promptly at eleven."

Raylene again awarded the man one of her beautiful smiles. "I'll be ready."

Joe rushed through the remainder of the people, not listening to names or saying any more than he had to. For no apparent reason he suddenly felt angry and hurt . . . perhaps even betrayed.

As soon as the last person had walked away, he headed into the back room, shrugged out of his suit coat, and tossed it onto the table.

Raylene followed him in silence, but Joe passed through the kitchen and out the rear door. He went to the back of the wagon and dug through his saddlebags to find the bottle of whiskey he usually carried. Returning to the kitchen, he took a cup down from the cupboard and poured himself a small portion. Raylene frowned at his behavior while he took a couple of sips.

"I'm not a drinking man," he explained, wincing at the harsh burn along his throat, "but I sure need something to steady my nerves."

"You deserve to be congratulated, Joe," she praised him rather than criticizing his taking a drink. "But I admit, you surprised me. When did you think of the punishment for Mr. Boggs?"

Joe took another sip and tried not to gag. He really hated the taste of hard liquor and only carried a bottle to use for social encounters. "I apologize for not doing what you told me," he said, not answering the question. "I was afraid a fine would only make things worse. If Boggs has been wasting his money gambling and drinking, the last thing he needed was to pay a fine."

"I must say, Joe" — Raylene was deadly serious — "I have never heard of a judge imposing such a sentence."

"Yeah, well, it was all I could think of." He still had a bitter taste in his mouth. "I still don't know nothing about being a judge."

"Perhaps not, but you did a first-rate job of handling the situation. I can't imagine Father doing any better. The verdict and punishment were fair and necessary and completely unexpected."

"Dumb luck," he said, still angry.

"What's gotten into you?" Raylene wanted

to know. "You were cheerful and confident a few minutes ago. I was proud of you."

Joe flinched. "Proud? Of me?"

"Yes, of the way you handled the court and that fancy lawyer. You did more than entertain a hearing, you dispensed actual justice. I — I am very impressed, especially when we had only a couple of hours to prepare."

Joe hated the way she was so blasted complimentary. He wanted to lash out at her. He ought to tell her what a fool she was for agreeing to have lunch with some jasper she had just met. Why did she have to be so nice?

"Are you hungry?" Raylene asked after Joe did not offer to speak. "I can fix something."

"No need going to any trouble on my account. I'm not used to eating more than one or two meals a day."

"All right," she said, still regarding him with an odd sort of bewilderment. "Will you be here for supper? I was going to make a stew."

"I'll probably be around," Joe said, again wondering why he felt so mixed up. "I need to continue working on the corral fence, fill the new watering trough, and round up some feed for the horses."

"We'll eat about sunset," Raylene told him. Then she went into the bedroom to change out of her courtroom dress and get back into work clothes.

Joe took the last sip of liquor. It burned the lining of his throat and certainly did not make him feel any better. He gathered up the bottle and his jacket and went outside to the wagon. He climbed up into the back and changed into his own work clothes. He felt the need for exertion, for exercise. He had a bottled-up feeling that needed an outlet.

Even as he finished changing clothes and climbed back out of the wagon, he wondered what was eating at him. So what if a sweet-talking, educated fellow had asked Myra to lunch? It was only part of the game they were playing, wasn't it?

The rationalization didn't help. He still felt as if he had swallowed a badger whole and it was trying mightily to escape through his chest.

"Should have known better than to let myself get close to a gal like Raylene," he muttered to himself. "There can't be anything worse or harder on a man than a good woman!"

Chase Estcott kept watch over his brother

and Myra until they were back in their large house. He closed his eyes yet could still see the natural sway of Myra when she walked. Her skin was smooth and flawless, as soft as the cheek of a newborn baby. She walked with a natural grace and had the poise of a princess. Everything about her was perfection.

"And she belongs to Dunn," he muttered to himself. "Everything in this life worth having belongs to my big brother!"

"You say something, Chase?" Vern asked, standing a few feet away.

"Cursing the woman who bore me, Vern," he replied acidly. "I can't help but think, had I been born first, I'd be walking around in Dunn's shoes."

Vern showed his mutt-like grin. "It's Myra again, ain't it."

The conclusion was not a question. Vern wasn't the brightest lamp on the wall, but even he knew that Chase wanted a woman he could never have. Rather than continue lusting after his brother's wife, Chase uttered a sigh.

"You seen Dunn and her talking to the judge. I'd wager my brother's decided to let the guy stay . . . and that judge is going to be trouble. You mind what I say, Vern. He's trouble — I can feel it."

Vern gently rubbed the dark bruise near his left temple. "You don't have to tell me," he snorted. "First time I catch him without his gun, I'll tear him to pieces like he was made of paper."

Chase thought for a moment. Dunn had warned them off for the day, but he hadn't said a word about tomorrow.

"The man isn't alone very often, Vern. It will be hard to catch him at the right time."

"I seen Brock smooth-talking his sister. I'll bet they made some kind of plans together." At Chase's curious look, he added, "I could tell by the way Brock's face lit up when he walked away from her. The guy had a grin on his face that about swallowed up both of his ears."

"If that's the case, the judge might end up alone tomorrow sometime. Brock isn't the kind of man to sit around and wait. And his newspaper is due out in two days. If he used the excuse of an interview or something, he'll have gotten her hooked for something tomorrow."

"I'll be watching," Vern said. "When the chance comes, I'll sure enough rearrange the judge's pretty face."

"Watch how you handle it," Chase warned the big man. "If you don't make it a fair fight, you could end up in jail."

"You're talking like the man is going to be walking and talking when the fight is over." Vern sneered. "After I use him like a broom and sweep the floor with him, he ain't gonna be sending no one to jail."

"I like the sound of that, Vern. If Dunn says anything, I'll tell him I gave you the go-ahead to get even. After all, the judge did hit you when you weren't expecting it."

Vern nodded, then changed the subject. "It doesn't seem fair, Chase. You do more work than Dunn. You take all the risks down here on the streets. How come you still have to do everything your brother says?"

"Because his name is on all of the ownership papers in Gold Butte, Vern. He has title to the Silver Lady Mine, the casino, the company store, the smelter, and the railroad. He owns everything, and all I am is a glorified hired hand."

"Still don't seem fair."

"Only the rich and powerful think life is fair, Vern. Put them in an ordinary man's shoes, and they would bawl like spoiled-brat babies."

Vern laughed. "You got that right, Chase. You shore do."

"Let's go play some cards. Dunn said to take the day off."

The bigger man shook his head. "Every

time I play cards with you, I go home broke. I think I'll go fishing instead."

Chase chuckled and punched Vern playfully. "Never figured you for a coward."

Vern displayed a good-natured grin. "Ain't being a coward to admit another man is better at cards than you are . . . and you're about the best I ever run across."

"Right you are, big guy. I'll see you later."

Vern headed toward the bunkhouse behind the jail, where he, Keno, and Pike shared quarters. At night one of them would take his turn sleeping in the jail, so they would be handy if someone needed the law. Such had been the case last night, when Keno had been taking his turn.

"Stupid clown," Chase muttered. Had Keno settled the family squabble with a firm warning or by giving Boggs a couple of lumps, there would have been no need for the judge to get involved. Now Gordon Stanfield had won over a good many allies. Running him out of town was no longer an option, and Dunn was not going to be happy when Vern stomped on him.

Chase dismissed the concern. Vern owed the judge a beating. No one in town was going to deny that Stanfield had that much coming. With a smile of anticipation he wandered off toward the saloon. If he was lucky there might be a couple of suckers to fleece at the gambling tables. Vern was right not to play cards with him, not if he wanted to keep any spending money in his pocket. There wasn't a man in town who could best Chase at cards. Not one.

The dishes had been cleaned and put away before Raylene took a timepiece from her purse and looked at it. "It's getting late. I need to get my sleep so my eyes aren't red and tired tomorrow."

"Yeah." Joe did not hide his sarcasm. "It wouldn't do for you to look less than perfect for the newspaper man."

A set of frown lines furrowed Raylene's brow. "He's going to print a story about us, about having a fair and impartial judge in town. It suits our purpose."

"I reckon I ain't so blind as to see whose purpose is being served," Joe continued bitterly.

"There is nothing improper about my having lunch with Mr. Brock."

"I'm supposed to be the judge here, so why didn't he ask me to come along?" Joe wanted to know. "I mean, I should think the story would be about both of us, right?"

"You're an outlaw!" she retorted, her temper flaring. "Would you like him to also letter?"

"That ain't the point," Joe shot back. "He should be writing a story about the town of Gold Butte having a new judge and court-house. The man didn't even pause to spit on my shoes; he passed me right by and latched on to you like the ace of his trump suit."

A light of understanding entered Raylene's eyes. "You're jealous," she declared. "That's it, isn't it?"

"Jealous?" Joe was incredulous. "Why would I be jealous of some no-account gossip-printer?"

"Because he is refined and educated. You begrudge his being a writer while you are trying to learn the meaning of words like *litigation*."

Joe had taken all he could stand. Let Raylene go have lunch with some fast-talking joker. She thought he was jealous of Steve Brock because he was educated and literate? Well, maybe that was partly true, but it still didn't turn all of the cards face up. If Raylene had been fifty years old and posing as his mother, there was no way that newshound would have asked her to have lunch with him. Talk about not being able to read! She was the one who was as blind as a tree stump! He rose from the table and picked up his hat.

"I'll say good night, ma'am," he told her. "I'm tired of this here conversation, and you need your beauty rest."

"It's not *ma'am!*" she reminded him sternly.

"Yes, *ma'am,*" he retorted critically. "Tonight it is!" Then he left the room and went out the back door and into the darkness. He climbed up into the back of the wagon and sprawled onto his bed. Rather than remove his boots and gun, he lay there for a time and stared at the canvas ceiling overhead.

He hated feeling inadequate and stupid. He never should have agreed to this pretense. While sitting at a card table, he always kept a cool head and remained in control. He was readily accepted for what he was — a professional gambler. He didn't have to prove anything to anyone. He did his talking and earned respect with his mastery of the game. Since meeting Raylene, he had been out of step with the world, unable to do much of anything right. To make things worse, she caused him to have inner feelings that ran the deck from deuce to king. A word of praise from her, and he was floating among the clouds. With her criticism, he felt the world crash down upon his shoulders.

And this new sensation was the worst. Whether it was jealousy, envy, or what, it caused a gnawing discomfort in the pit of his stomach, as if he had swallowed a handful of barbed wire.

"I commence to see why people pray," he murmured, staring up at the dark canvas overhead. "There comes a time when a man needs to tell someone his troubles. I reckon having a god serves a necessary purpose, whether He is real or not."

CHAPTER SIX

Myra didn't partake of breakfast and was not an early riser, so Dunn usually ate his morning meal at either the hotel or the Grub House cafe. He had finished the meal and was sipping his second cup of coffee, when Chase entered the room.

Chase spotted Dunn and came over to his table. He didn't speak until he had pulled out a chair and sat down. "I reckon I know your verdict on our new judge," he said thickly.

"The man showed some insight with his decision, Chase. I don't believe he will cause us any serious problems."

"You're running with blinders on, big brother," Chase said back. "I'll wager the man makes a nuisance of himself before the month is out."

"Could be," Dunn allowed, "but we'll wait and see."

"I seen you and Myra talking to him after

the trial. It appeared your wife was real impressed."

"Are you trying to make a point?"

Chase shrugged. "Only that Myra pretty much handles your reins these days. I figure if she said the judge can stay, you went along with it."

Dunn narrowed his gaze. "You enjoy tossing Myra in my face, but she's not my boss or keeper; she's my wife, my life partner."

Chase raised his hands to ward off the rebuttal. "Hey, I'd be the first to admit that she's a lot of woman, Dunn. Fact is, if she wasn't married to you, I sure wouldn't throw rocks at her to keep her at a distance."

Dunn sipped his coffee and did not respond to the comment.

"My worry is it that Myra will cloud your opinion, such as your honest take on this new judge." Chase returned to the original subject.

Dunn was still weighing what Chase had said. He knew his brother blamed Myra for coming between them, but was it more than that? She was a beautiful woman for any town or city. Here in Gold Butte she might be deemed a goddess.

"Hey!" Chase spoke a bit louder. "You here with me, Dunn, or have you gone fishing?"

Dunn recovered his wits. "The judge didn't say a word about the miners or taxes or anything else. My impression is that he was uncomfortable meeting so many people up close and personal."

"Maybe he's hiding something," Chase concluded. "You think there's more to his background than being a simple judge?"

"I don't know," Dunn evaded. "When have you ever attended a court hearing where the judge wore a gun?"

"You could count all the times I've been in a courtroom on one hand," Chase said. "But you've got a point. I don't remember ever seeing a judge wearing a gun, especially not the way that jasper wears his. And we know the man is capable of getting it out of the holster and into use right quick."

"I overheard Steve Brock ask the judge's sister to join him for lunch. If you're so concerned, perhaps you should have a few words with Brock. He can question the girl about Gordon's background and put your mind at ease."

"Be just as easy to run him out of town," Chase said. "Then we wouldn't have to worry one way or the other."

"We'll try it my way first," Dunn replied, taking a sip of his coffee. "I rather liked the way he handled the business with Boggs."

Chase frowned, but he didn't argue. He pushed back and got to his feet. "You're the boss," he said.

Funny, but his brother seemed to be saying that a lot lately. Each time, Dunn wondered if it would be the moment of challenge. Chase was hungry for more — more power, more wealth, more authority. He rose from the table and sauntered out of the cafe without a backward look.

Dunn might have worried more about his brother's attitude, but there were other things on his mind. He was growing tired of managing an empire. He would like to find a place where he could enjoy life, where he and Myra could live in comfort and get together with friends for social gatherings. She wanted to travel more, visit some of the larger cities and attend the theater or shop in fashionable shops. His primary goal in life was to please her, and the thought of leaving the business here at Gold Butte had crossed his mind often. But Chase was not the man to manage his affairs. Chase was wild and impulsive, too quick to take the violent road to crush his every adversary. Most towns, like the government, need two sides, a positive and negative view for any major argument or decision. They need balance. Chase didn't want to debate any issue; he threw muscle and threats at the issue until it was decided in his favor. He was not a suitable replacement to handle the daily chores and business ends of things.

Reflecting upon whether the judge should stay in town, Dunn remembered looking into the man's eyes. Stanfield had met his gaze with a cool evaluation, revealing no animosity or suspicion. Tom Lawson had obviously laid out Gold Butte and how it worked, yet Stanfield's look had been veiled and unreadable. Dunn had a feeling the judge was neither a fool nor a man who accepted anyone's word at face value. He would take a wait-and-see approach with Judge Stanfield.

Being a renowned bounty hunter, Taggart had a reputation as a man who would do a special chore when the price was right. He had ridden over a hundred miles for this job and was eager to get started. Waiting for the mayor to make his speech, Taggart glanced over the Wanted poster on Joe Bratt.

Conroy Masterson was the type of man he had worked for many times. Taggart neither liked nor respected them privately, but when the money was right, it made not the slightest difference. Conroy, like most of the others, had attained a lofty position, and it had gone to his head. Wealth and power was a club, something a rich man wielded to knock down those who opposed him. Laws weren't intended for such elite people but were necessary to keep the poor and less deserving folks in line.

"You see the position I'm in here, Taggart," Conroy was saying. "All I want is justice for the killing of my brother. He went looking for a thief, trying only to get his money back, and some quick-trigger gunman killed him."

"I understand," Taggart said. "Only one way to get justice done."

"That's right," Conroy agreed. "I knew you would understand. The posse lost him and isn't interested in trying to find him again. They've stopped looking."

"I don't work for the law, Masterson. I work for money."

"The reward still goes," Conroy assured him. "One thousand dollars . . . paid privately."

Taggart lifted a corner of his mouth in a mirthless grin. "With no 'dead or alive' attached to this here bounty, right? I mean, the man's got to be dead, correct?"

Conroy cleared his throat. "I believe we understand each other."

"Where did the posse lose him?"

"On a rock mesa thirty miles due south of Gold Butte."

"They look for him in Gold Butte?"

"The posse split up and checked the nearby towns and ranches. He didn't show up the next day, so they came home. They claim he probably died out in the wilderness."

"If he did, I'll find his body."

"That's all I want, proof that he's dead."

Taggart gave a nod of his head and turned for the door. "Have the money ready," he said over his shoulder to Conroy. "I'll be back in a week or two."

Joe avoided Raylene the next day. They shared an uncomfortably quiet breakfast, and he went out back to work on the corral. A few hours later he spied her and Steve Brock leaving together. Raylene looked as striking as a decorated Christmas tree, while the newspaper man held his head high, as cocky and proud as the only rooster in the barnyard.

Joe couldn't pin down the reason, but he hated the idea of Raylene's going off with Brock. Be it lunch or a picnic in the hills, he simply didn't care for the two of them being off alone together. They would laugh and talk — all smart and educated — and

Raylene was bound to be impressed by Brock's use of fancy words and his position as editor of the town newspaper.

Joe muttered an oath under his breath and went to the wagon. He took out one of Gordon's law books and began to thumb through it. When he reached a page filled with legal terminology, he paused to read some definitions. While many were confusing and hard to understand, he found a couple of terms and paragraphs interesting. The more he read, the more a plan began to form in his head.

Joe went inside and rounded up a pen and paper. With the book at hand, he began to write a letter. It wasn't easy to put the words onto paper, but he took his time and looked up the spelling for some of the harder ones. Fortunately, the book had a section in back to explain certain words and terms. It took the better part of an hour, but Joe was satisfied with the result. He addressed two different letters and took them over to Tom Lawson, who was also the town postmaster.

"Good day to you, Judge," Tom greeted him.

"Tom," Joe returned. "Like to mail a couple letters."

"Sure thing," Tom said. "You have good timing. The narrow-gauge is going down to the main line today. The mail gets transferred onto the train there and is taken to Denver." He looked at the address on the letter Joe handed him. "This ought to reach its destination in three or four days."

"That's good. This second one goes to Denver too, but I don't have the address."

Tom looked at the name and smiled. "Not a problem, Judge. I know how to get that one into the right hands."

Joe watched as Tom scribbled a couple of lines under the name. "That's it?"

"I'm certain the postal service knows where to find a gent with a title like his."

There was no one else in the store at the moment, so Tom could give Joe all of his attention. Once Joe had paid for the postage and Tom had added the letters to a mail sack, the storekeeper turned serious.

"I saw your sister walking down to the hotel eatery with Steve Brock."

"Yeah, he wanted an interview with her."

Tom's head bobbed up and down. "I'm not surprised. It isn't every day a woman gets to practice law in an actual courtroom."

"That was his line as well."

Tom laughed. "Being that your sister is the prettiest single woman in town, you think that might have added to his desire for an interview?"

"It crossed my mind."

"Steve is an all right sort of guy. I'm sure he will be a perfect gentleman."

"If he ain't, I'll sure enough learn him some manners."

Tom chuckled again. "Spoken like a true protective brother."

Joe had to smile too. "Maybe a little too protective — is that your thinking?"

"I'd say your sister is smart enough to recognize a polecat from a house cat, Judge. Steve won't get out of line with someone like her."

"Thanks for telling me about him, Tom. It puts my mind at ease."

"Anytime, Judge," Tom said with a smile. "We're mighty glad to have you here in Gold Butte."

Joe said his farewell and started back to the courthouse. When he reached the center of the main street in town, he saw Steve Brock leading Raylene in the direction of his office. She happened to see Joe and gave him a wave. It appeared she would not be coming back for a while. Joe lifted a hand so she would know he had seen her and then shuffled back to the front of the old barn.

He paused before entering, looking up at the white cross on the building. Maybe

Raylene would flutter her tantalizing eyelashes at Brock and get him to replace the cross with a sign that designated the ex-barn, ex-church as now being a courthouse.

"Excuse me, Judge?" A female voice broke into his pondering.

Joe started, yanked brusquely from his solitary world, and swung his attention to the intruder. She was a mature-looking woman, dressed in tattered but clean clothes, with her hair tucked up under a Quaker-style bonnet. She offered him a timid smile, which accentuated the lines in her matronly yet amicable face.

"You don't know me, Judge," she began, "but I'm a friend of Mrs. Boggs. I had children to tend, so I wasn't here during court yesterday, but Mary was very impressed. She thinks you might have saved their marriage."

"Little early to start spreading rumors like that, ma'am," Joe replied. "That why you stopped by, to give me a pat on the back for doing my job?"

The woman looked too embarrassed to continue. "Actually, the reason I've come" — she inhaled deeply and blurted out — "was to ask if you might be in need of hiring a little work done." A trace of color crept into the woman's cheeks. Joe got the impression that this was not a woman who often asked anyone for anything. Regardless, she continued. "I would offer to volunteer my services for free, but my husband was hurt in a mining accident a short while back. It will be another week or two before he can return to work, and we have two children. The wages my Greg earns in the mines haven't allowed for us to set aside very much for this kind of emergency. With him unable to work, I . . ." Her voice cracked, and she had to pause long enough to swallow. "Anyway, I thought perhaps you could use some help in fixing up the courtroom."

Joe was stunned and a little out of his depth. He had never before been in a position where anyone had asked him for anything. He often left extra money for a meal or a room and usually tipped the hostler or liveryman. But this, someone asking him for a job? A job so she could help feed her family? It was completely unexpected.

At his delay in answering, the woman hurried on with her proposal. "My father made furniture for a living back in Pennsylvania. I used to help him with his work when I was growing up. Over the years I've made cushions and miscellaneous pieces of furniture for our family and others."

"I see," Joe said, not really understanding

150

where the conversation was going.

"It would only take a little money," the woman hurried to explain, "and I could greatly improve the looks and comfort of the benches for the court audience."

That sounded promising. "What did you say your name was?" he asked.

"Kate Miller," she replied.

"Okay, Mrs. Miller, show me what you have in mind."

Kate went with Joe into the barn structure and entered the makeshift courtroom. As he paced at her side, she went about the meeting room, pointing here and there as she spoke. By the time she finished, he was impressed.

"How long do you think it would take?" Joe asked, once she had covered everything she had in mind.

"If I was to have my kids and sister-in-law help, the four of us could probably do it all in one afternoon."

"What about wages?" he asked. "How much would all of this cost?"

"There would be the price of the material, the wood stain, and a few other items for cleaning."

"Yes, besides the supplies?"

Kate appeared fearful to ask. "I dunno." She licked her lips and appeared to summon her courage. "Four of us working about a half day — does two or three dollars sound fair?"

Joe about laughed in her face over such a small amount. However, he could see she was deadly serious, so he put on his poker face, pretending to mull over the number instead.

"It's like I told you," Kate hurried to clarify, "if Greg hadn't been injured, I would have offered to help with sprucing up the courtroom for free. It's just that we don't have . . ."

"Tell you what, Mrs. Miller," Joe said, preventing her from humbling herself further. "If you can do all of the work you've mapped out and finish it this afternoon, I figure it would be worth at least ten dollars."

"Ten dollars!" She was flabbergasted. "That's extremely generous."

"Are you game?" Joe asked. "You won't have all that much time."

"It's barely noon," she said, her mind quickly outlining the chores. "Yes, with several of us working together, I'm sure we can get it all done today!"

Joe smiled. "I'll tell Tom to give you whatever you need at the store."

Then it happened, the strangest thing Joe

had ever encountered. The woman grabbed his hand with both of her own, raised it up to her lips, and actually kissed it. "You are a good man," she said, tears glistening in her eyes. "Thank you, Judge. Thank you with all of my heart."

Joe stood, mouth agape, as the woman whirled about and rushed from the barn. When she was out of sight, Joe recovered his wits enough to close his mouth.

The internal agony he had felt over Raylene's being off with Brock was pushed aside. He felt an odd tingle that seemed to warm him inside. It was like being a little tipsy from too much drink, yet his head was clear. He had never received that kind of thanks before, not in his entire life.

He smiled and spoke aloud. "So, this is what doing a good deed is all about. Hotdang! I've really been missing something."

Steve was entertaining and widely educated. In some ways, he reminded Raylene of her father. He tended to take matters seriously, and the newspaper was the most important thing in his life.

Raylene had been forced to associate with people from all walks of life, ever since she was old enough to talk. It was fortunate Gordon had been worldly, as the discourse between herself and Steve covered weather patterns, world events, the politics of the nation, and a number of problems facing the local populace.

Their lunch together had been mostly to get acquainted. Once she had agreed to see his workplace, Steve proudly showed her around his office and demonstrated how the printing equipment worked. He had a great variety of reading materials, books on many subjects, including beginning readers for school. When she asked about that, he laughed.

"This office is the closest thing we have to a library. Over the years I've picked up books at auctions or even paid a few cents for a copy to help out a traveler. I am optimistic there will be an actual school here in Gold Butte one of these days, so I bought some children's readers."

"That's very thoughtful of you."

"You're welcome to borrow any of the books I have."

Raylene marveled over the many titles and looked through his stack of journals and magazines from Eastern publishers. She considered making an excuse to leave, but Steve insisted upon sitting down and going through some of his collection. After sifting through a second pile, he produced a stack of photographs and drawings, most from some kind of publication or another and a few of his own. Finally, it was on to his weekly newspaper, which he had put out since arriving in town. As they went through the materials together, she was amazed at some of the stories and articles.

"See here" — he pointed to one page — "this was a sad affair, the death of four miners when a tunnel collapsed. My story was carried in a Denver newspaper and one back east." He shuffled through another few papers and held up another. "This ought to interest you. It's a short narrative about your brother's predecessor and how he left town without even bothering to unpack. I'm surprised you didn't encounter the same sort of intimidation."

Raylene scanned the article. She well remembered the reception she and Joe had received, but Joe had handled it with very little effort. She would have mentioned it, but then Steve would want to print something about it. The less printed about Joe in the paper, the better.

"And now I want some information for the story about you," Steve said. "Have you attended one of the coed or women's colleges and studied law, or did you learn everything from your brother?"

"It was my father, Gordon senior, who taught me most of what I have learned. Other kids are taught to read from early readers, like the few you have here, but I learned to read from law books. My father had a never-ending thirst for information and discovery behind the meaning and letter of the law. I became his personal clerk when I was ten or eleven and took notes and sorted through texts to provide him with the necessary research for his rulings."

"I know that many lawyers are given their license by simply appearing before a judge or even gain their credentials via the appointment of a mayor or city official. Was that the case with you?"

"I suppose you could say I was appointed to the position by my father, but I never had the opportunity to practice law until Jo . . . uh, my brother," she quickly corrected, "appointed me to prosecute the case against Mr. Boggs."

"You did a superb job," Steve praised. "Calling Dunn Estcott to the stand was a brilliant strategy. Lavar Crump could hardly attack the testimony of his own boss on cross-examine!"

"It was fortunate Mr. Estcott was so forthcoming. It gave my brother the evidence he needed to rule on the case. That was my intention."

Steve jotted down a few lines on a piece of paper, and Raylene glanced out the window. She gasped in surprise, realizing the sun was about to set, and dug out her timepiece.

"Do I have the right time?" she asked. "Have I really spent the entire afternoon at your office?"

"It has been the best six hours I've had since my arrival in Gold Butte," Steve proclaimed. "You are indeed an extraordinary woman. I will set print for the article concerning the trial this very evening. I'm sure you will be pleased."

"I didn't intend to take up your whole day," she said, rising from the chair she had been occupying for several hours. "You've been a most gracious host."

Steve showed a wide smile. "It is not often I get to entertain a beautiful woman. I assure you, the pleasure was mine."

"I really have to be getting back. I promised my brother I would bake him some fresh rolls for supper." She sighed. "Guess that isn't going to happen tonight."

"Speaking of your brother" — Steve's smile vanished — "I am somewhat surprised that Gordon junior seems — how shall I put it? — considerably less educated than you."

Raylene worded her reply carefully. "It is not a requirement to have earned honors at a renowned college for a man to become a judge. As you already pointed out, the appointment is based upon many factors."

"Of course." Steve seemed to dismiss the subject. "It only struck me odd that you seem the more scholarly one in the family."

"Gordon didn't start out with a desire to become a judge. He spent a number of years in the gambling profession before he accepted the position." She summoned forth a doleful sigh to cover the half truth. "In essence, it was the death of our father that prompted him to truly assume the role of judge."

Steve displayed a keen interest. "I am sorry I never got to meet your father. He sounds like quite a man."

"Yes, he was," Raylene replied.

"I sense you are rather protective of your brother," Steve said. "And I noticed his reaction to my asking you to share a meal with me today. He seems equally protective of you."

Raylene didn't care for his observation. "It's perfectly natural for a brother and sister to look out for each other's interest."

Steve bore into her with a curious scrutiny. "Is that all it is?"

A warning flag zipped up Raylene's worry pole, but she hid the concern. "What do you mean?"

"Something about your brother doesn't fit, Raylene." He either didn't notice or ignored her tight frown at his using her given name. She had not granted him that privilege yet. He ventured recklessly forward with his concerns. "Tom and Ellen shared information with me about their requesting another judge. The reply stated we could expect someone with a great deal of experience, a man who had been on the bench for many years." Steve paused to let the words sink in. "Gordon does not seem old enough to have been a circuit judge for all that long."

Raylene couldn't tell the complete truth, so she decided to bend it a little for the second time. "You are right, Mr. Brock. My father was originally slated to serve as the new judge in Gold Butte," she explained. "When he died rather suddenly, my brother volunteered to take his place. This is Gordon's first genuine appointment. We thought it better if the people in town assumed he had a degree of experience." Then, more pointedly, she added, "And you saw for

159

yourself how he took control of the hearing yesterday and managed a just and fair sentence."

"Yes, I was impressed, and, again, I am sorry about the death of your father," Steve replied.

"His loss is still quite painful to both of us."

"You were fortunate to have your brother standing by, ready to accept a new appointment."

"Yes, it was most opportune," Raylene replied a bit curtly. "Now, if the interrogation part of our afternoon is over, I should be getting back."

"I didn't mean to come on like a Pinkerton Eye or something," Steve hastily backpedaled. "I'm a reporter, so I tend to seek out the background to any story I come across."

"You flatter me." Raylene grew caustic. "Referring to me as a *story*."

"No!" Steve was trapped by his own smug skepticism. "I was speaking of your brother. He's the one I was curious about."

"I must leave now," Raylene declared, turning for the door. "Thank you for the offer to lend me a book. Perhaps I will take you up on it sometime."

"Raylene, don't be upset with me. I only

wanted —"

"And," she interrupted his apology, "I think it only proper that we remain on a formal basis, *Mr.* Brock."

Steve appeared devastated by the turn of events. "Certainly, Miss Stanfield, it wasn't my intention to be presumptuous. I thought we were becoming friends."

"Of course," she said, but she did not retract the statement. "It's getting late, and I've got to run to the store and pick up something for supper."

Steve hung his head like a whipped dog. "All right, Miss Stanfield." He was quietly submissive. "Let me say again what a pleasure it's been to have had you spend today with me."

Raylene gave him a curt nod and left the office.

CHAPTER SEVEN

Joe took a short survey of the room, impressed by the job the team of workers had done. Kate had purchased everything they needed from the mercantile and arrived with both of her children — one was a boy of thirteen and the other a girl of eleven — and she had also brought along her sister-in-law, Marge, to help. Marge and the two kids first cleaned and then applied an even coat of varnish to the benches. During that time Kate folded, cut, and measured lengths of several durable blankets. As soon as the stain began to dry, she and Marge worked together. They wrapped a layer of batting inside the material and then tucked and folded the pre-fitted blankets neatly along the bench seats. Kate hammered tacks along the underside of the railing, front and back, to secure the padding in place. When they were finished, matching cushions covered every one of the benches.

The kids had continued to clean the place from walls to floor, taking out piles of trash and leftover junk, some of it back from the days when the place had been used as a barn. The entire crew worked diligently and completed the job in just over four hours.

Joe took a walk around the room and commented favorably on their handiwork. Then he stopped to face them and pulled some money from his pocket. He handed Kate the ten dollars he had promised, but he also handed the other woman and both kids a dollar each.

"You did a great job," he told them all. "I really do appreciate your efforts."

Kate stood breathless after receiving the money. "Thank you so much, Your Honor," she gushed. "You have no idea how much this will help my family."

"Yes." Marge also spoke up. "We had hoped we could earn a dollar or two for a whole day's work. But this is really too much for . . ."

Joe waved a hand to dismiss further discussion. "I had some luck at a poker game last night."

"It's still exceptionally generous."

"One thing I'm curious about, ladies," he said. "What kind of wages do your men earn in the mines?"

Kate answered. "For a ten-hour day, our husbands earn two dollars in cash and another dollar credited toward our rent and the tools and supplies they use in the mine."

Joe immediately decided that being a gambler had been a better choice for him than hard rock mining. He asked, "The miners have to buy their own tools?"

"Yes, they do. And each man is required to make so many inches in digging each day. If he doesn't meet his quota, they cut his pay by half. That means the men need sharp drill bits and good hammers. The explosives don't come cheap either."

Joe shook his head in appreciation. "Takes a special kind of man to handle a job like that."

"It is a living for men with no hankering for farming or ranching," Marge said.

"Has either of your men worked at other mines?"

"Yes." Kate was the one to reply. "But they're all about the same. Our men work till they're about to drop to earn a day's wages. It's a hard life."

"Thanks again for the wonderful job," he told the four of them. "It makes the place look much more like a real courtroom."

Kate flashed him a smile. Her teeth were not in the best of shape, but she had proven she was a good worker. "It's to you we owe thanks, Judge," she said. "I'll be sure and keep you in my prayers."

Then the small work force left the meeting room. Joe stood for a long moment and inhaled the lingering smell of the varnish. It had a newness to it, as did the appearance of the entire room. It still looked like a barn on the outside, but the work had made a big improvement on the inside.

The entrance door suddenly opened, and Joe looked over to see Bulldog Vern's bulk as he stormed into the room.

"All right, you underhanded sneak," the big man threatened. "We're going to have us a go right now!"

Joe looked past him, but the man had obviously come alone.

"Are you here as a deputy, Vern, or is this personal business?"

The man ignored his question, lifted his balled fists, and moved closer. "I owe you for clubbing me with your gun." He sneered. "And you ain't going to take me by surprise this time."

Joe started toward him but held up his hands, palms outward, in a show of peace. "Look around you, Vern," he said. "A couple of the miners' wives and kids just finished cleaning up the place. You don't want to ruin all their hard work."

Vern snarled back, "Their work don't make me no never-mind! I come to square a debt."

Joe continued to move toward the man until he was at arm's length. "Are you sure we can't talk this out without resorting to a fight?"

"Not hardly, Judge. I'm gonna beat you like a dirty rug!"

Joe nodded toward the entrance. "What about the painting of the president above the door? Are you intending to start a fight right in front of the leader of our country?"

Vern unwisely glanced over his shoulder. "I didn't see no —"

Joe whipped out his right leg and kicked Vern squarely in the knee. "Okay," Joe said, as the man howled in pain, "if there's no talking you out of it."

Vern clutched his leg with both hands. That allowed Joe to slip in and snap off a sharp jab, striking Vern sharply between the eyes — not too hard, just enough to make his eyes water.

Vern hobbled about, blinded by the single punch. A push from Joe sent him reeling backward, where he slammed against a wall. He planted his uninjured leg for support and raised his guard, ready to fight.

But Joe didn't swing at him. Instead, he kicked him soundly in his good knee. The pain caused Vern to cry out again, and he sank to the floor. Throwing up both hands, he covered his head, expecting to be battered while helpless.

The blows never came.

"I don't want to fight you, Vern," Joe told him quietly, seriously. "We both know you're a whole lot tougher than I am."

After a full minute, Vern peeked out from behind his arms to look at Joe. Seeing he wasn't going to be beaten while helpless, he began to gingerly rub both of his knees.

"You could have put a lot of hurt on me whilst I was down here on the ground," Vern said. "Whupping me would make you out to be the big man around town. Ain't but one or two guys in the country who could go toe-to-toe with me."

"I don't have any quarrel with you, Vern. I only kicked you so you wouldn't bust me into a dozen tiny pieces."

"Hurts like hell."

"Yeah," Joe agreed, "it's no fun getting smacked in the knee."

"I wanted to get even for the clout you gave me with your pistol."

"It was nothing personal," Joe explained. "Had Keno been the closer man, I'd have hit him instead. I knew I didn't have a chance against the two of you."

"Well, this is going to look bad for me, limping out of here without giving you what-for."

Joe frowned. "You mean you bragged to some other men about what you were going to do to me?"

"No" — he shrugged — "only mentioned to Chase I might stop by. We ain't supposed to do nothing to you without orders."

Joe didn't ask who the order would have come from, though the Estcott brothers jumped to mind. Instead, he offered a grin as a peace offering. "If Chase doesn't know you came in here, he won't know we had this conversation, Vern. And I won't be telling anyone about our little talk."

"You mean it?"

"Vern," Joe said dryly, "you're in a court-room, and I'm a judge. If I wanted to charge you with attempted assault, I would have you tossed into jail. I've no reason to stand here and lie to you."

Vern paused to rub the tender spot on the bridge of his nose. "How come you didn't hit me harder? Wide open like that, you could have just as easily broke my nose."

"Like I told you, I don't want to fight with you. I was only trying to slow you down until we could talk this out."

"My body is complaining about your kind of talking — still feels like a thousand bees are stinging both my knees. I'm thinking you're more than you claim, Judge."

"No one is exactly who he appears to be, Vern. Not me, not you."

"Me?"

"You give off the tough-guy act, but I believe you're a decent sort deep inside."

Vern snorted. "If my ma was alive, I reckon she would argue the point."

Joe chuckled. "I suppose mothers can have a narrow way of looking at things sometimes."

"Give me a hand up," Vern said, extending his arm.

Joe helped him to his feet but remained alert, ready to duck, in case the big guy was bluffing. If Vern was still intent upon breaking his bones, he would be in for the fight of his life.

Fortunately, Vern didn't offer to swing at him. He stood, a bit unsteady on his two aching knees, and gave his head a negative shake.

"I'm going to be walking around like I just sat astraddle a barrel cactus for the next day or two."

"For that, I beg your pardon, Vern."

"Yeah, I know, you was only stopping a fight betwixt the two of us."

"No hard feelings?" Joe asked, extending a hand in friendship.

Vern studied him for a long moment. "If the boss says to crush you like a dry biscuit, that's what I'll do." He scowled at Joe, but he did appear perplexed and somewhat hesitant. "Personally, I reckon you ain't a bad sort. You had me down and could have done me some real damage and earned a reputation at the same time. Far as I'm concerned, you and me are square."

Joe shook his hand and then watched him make his exit. He let out a sigh of relief when the door closed. However, he didn't have time to pat himself on the back, as another person appeared at the doorway. This time it was Raylene.

She hurried into the room, a small bag in her hand and a frantic look on her face. When she saw Joe standing there, her expression turned to puzzlement.

"That was Bulldog Vern," she exclaimed, "the man you hit with your gun!"

"You've a keen eye for recognizing people," he answered to the obvious.

She remained incredulous, looking him up and down as if expecting to see a mangled mess of blood and broken bones.

"I don't understand. You seem uninjured."

Joe remained nonchalant. "I kind of prefer it that way."

"But Vern, he . . ." Still confused and muddled, she blurted out, "Do you know what he said to me when we passed in the street just now?"

Joe felt a rush of warm blood surge through his veins. "What did he say?" he demanded to know. "If he made a crude remark, I'll . . ."

"He said 'Good day to you, ma'am'!" she declared.

Joe laughed. "I reckon it's okay if *he* calls you *ma'am.* After all, he ain't trying to pass himself off as your brother."

Raylene started to reply but then noticed the changes in the room. "What on earth?" she said, staring about in wonder. "What's been going on here?"

"Hope you approve." Joe could not hide his satisfaction. "I hired a little work done while you were out cavorting with your newspaper man."

Raylene returned her attention to him. "Cavorting?" She repeated his word, obviously surprised he would know and use it.

"You know, out doing the courting thing."

"Yes, I am familiar with the word, Joe." Then she waved a hand in a sweeping motion. "Don't tell me Mr. Vern was here to help clean the courtroom?"

"Why don't you take a seat?" he invited.

Raylene moved to the nearest bench. She tested the wood, making certain it was dry, and then sat down. "My, what an improvement!" she exclaimed. "It's actually comfortable."

"I reckon it won't be so hard on folks now to sit on those benches whenever court is in session."

"But how . . . who . . . ?"

"One of the miners' wives stopped by. Her man got hurt in a mining accident and can't work for a spell. She was needing to earn a little money, so she and her kids and one of her relations did all the work you see here."

"You hired them?"

"Yes, ma'am. It seemed the right thing to do."

"It's *Raylene,* not *ma'am!*" she corrected him sternly, but the wisp of a smile played upon her lips.

Joe's knees felt as if they would buckle. When she looked at him that way, it seemed the entire world emanated brightness and cheer. Suddenly lacking the power of speech, he grew rigid as a statue as Raylene came forward to stand in front of him. For a long moment he stood frozen, and she scrutinized him as if looking for something special.

"I continue to underestimate you, Joe." She finally broke the silence. "Every time I think I'm beginning to understand you, you up and surprise me."

He commanded his voice to obey. "Well, the benches did look more like they belonged at an auction yard than inside a courthouse. I think the sprucing-up is a big improvement."

"That isn't what I meant." At his continued bafflement, she explained. "You took it upon yourself to help out a person in need. It wasn't your job, and no one made you do it. You helped because you're a good person . . . the same way you came to help me and my father, the day I first met you."

"I'm only a gambler," Joe said, "playing a role."

"Of course you are," she retorted, though she again displayed a coy simper. She changed the subject. "Are you about ready to eat? I picked up some beans and bread at the store."

"Sounds like a feast for a king."

"I apologize," she said softly. "I was going to bake you fresh bread today. I believe the store-bought is several days old."

"That's okay. I'm not picky when it comes

to eating."

Raylene's eyes misted. "You deserve . . ." she began, but she did not finish the sentence. Instead, she did something completely beyond Joe's ability to reason. She ducked her head and began to cry.

"What's the matter?" Joe wanted to know, immediately concerned. "Did I do something wrong? Was it something I said?"

But Raylene took a step forward and put her arms around him. Joe stood there, his innards jumping about like a grasshopper in a sealed jar, while she hugged him tightly. More than a hug, she lowered her head onto his shoulder and wept.

Joe was utterly confounded by her behavior. He didn't know what else to do, so he stroked her back with one hand and cupped the back of her head with the other. It was the equivalent of trying to soothe a child's injury, but he had no idea where Raylene was hurting.

The lady regained her decorum after a few moments and stepped out of his grasp. When she looked up, her eyes were still misty, but she blinked against the last of her tears.

"I'm so sorry for such an outburst, Joe," she said. "I don't know what came over me."

"Are you okay?"

"Yes, I'm fine," Raylene replied, once again looking around the room. "The difference is quite impressive. If we build us a small platform and find a desk and chair, this place might actually pass for a courtroom. It was a good idea, hiring those people to spruce the place up."

"Really?"

"Yes, but I wish you had spoken to me about it first."

Joe shrugged. "You weren't here to ask."

"How much did all of this cost?"

"About fifteen dollars."

"Fifteen dollars!" Raylene exclaimed. "Did you have to give them so much?"

"A couple dollars went for the supplies," he explained. "Payment was only ten to Kate and a dollar each to the other three. It didn't seem right to have some of them working for nothing."

"Yes, but fifteen dollars!" Raylene complained a second time. "As you did not fine Mr. Boggs, we received exactly nothing from the court hearing. We can't afford to pay out more money than we take in."

"Don't worry about it." Joe dismissed her argument. "I ain't the sort to wander around busted down to my last penny."

Raylene looked ready to say something but thought better of it. When she did speak, it had nothing to do with his being a judge. "I'll prepare supper for us, unless you have other plans?"

"No, I'll see to the horses and wash up."

"It'll only take a few minutes. I didn't intend to be gone so long."

"Just as long as you had a good time," he said dispassionately.

"Actually, it was quite interesting. Steve has a wondrous library of books and magazines, along with scads of photographs and drawings. He insisted upon showing me about every newspaper he has printed since he arrived."

"Yeah, well, I'll see to the horses," Joe told her a second time, more than a little unhappy that she seemed to be enthralled by Steve Brock.

Raylene regarded him with a mystified look on her face, but Joe didn't stick around. He had done one thing Brock hadn't that day; he'd held Raylene in his arms. He didn't know what it meant, but it had sure felt good holding her close.

CHAPTER EIGHT

Taggart sat back in the trees and looked down upon the town of Gold Butte. He had spent several hours circling the mesa and following useless trails. The inquiries from the posse at nearby ranches or settlements had all returned the same answer: no one had seen hide nor hair of a gambler named Joe Bratt. That didn't satisfy Taggart.

As for the lack of a trail, that was nothing new for Taggart. He had a sixth sense about where his prey would run. From the point where Bratt's horse had vanished onto the rock mesa, he had studied every option. He put himself in place of his fugitive, possibly wounded, being hunted by a blood-hungry posse. The choices were limited, and the posse had readily exhausted all other avenues. Joe Bratt had to be in Gold Butte. It was the only possible direction he could have taken.

Taggart neck-reined his horse toward a

sheltered cove. He would get some rest, and, come dark, he would slip down into town and visit the saloons. A guarded question here or there, a dollar or two to loosen the right lips — if Bratt was in town, he would soon know it.

It had been a busy couple of days for Joe and Raylene. He finished mending the corral and arranged for the livery stable to provide feed for their animals. Raylene had begun to look over cross-filed claims from several prospectors and also intended to negotiate a dispute over water rights between two nearby ranches. She went over the material with Joe so he would be aware of the claims and her decisions.

Joe allowed her to do most of the office work, while he kept busy working around the courthouse and adding on a second bedroom. The weather could turn cold at any time, and he didn't want to be sleeping in the wagon when it started freezing at nights.

They adopted a pattern of eating a late breakfast and then would share a second meal in the early evening. After they cleaned and put away the dishes, Raylene would often read or review some of the cases. Joe didn't much care for the amount of reading and deciphering needed for such work. He often left her with her books and went to the casino for a friendly game of cards. Raylene was usually in bed before he returned, but this night she was waiting for him.

"Where have you been?" Raylene wanted to know.

"I was over at the Palace."

A frown immediately spread across her face. "You shouldn't be frequenting saloons and casinos all the time. It doesn't look proper."

"I mingle with the people," Joe replied. "It's not like I went out drinking hard liquor and chasing after" — he grinned — *"ladies of dubious honor."*

"How many times are you going to bring up my description of saloon women?"

Joe chuckled. "It does get a smile from most folks."

"I had a visitor while you were out," Raylene told him, changing the subject. "One of the local ranchers was in town and wanted to know if he could come courting."

Joe frowned. "What did you tell him?"

"I declined his offer, of course." She wrung her hands. "I knew there would be a shortage of women up here, but not to this extent. I've been approached by no fewer than a dozen men wanting to court me."

"And that's not counting those I sent away."

She gave him a questioning look. "You sent some away too?"

"There have been a couple proper sorts who figured I had to give my permission, what with my being your older brother."

"You never mentioned any suitors to me," she said. Subsequently, when he didn't offer to say anything more about it, she asked, "What did you tell them?"

"To get in line," he said, unable to hide his irritation. "If you allowed every guy who's come looking a day each for courting, it would be a year from next Christmas before you finished going through them all."

Raylene groaned. "I didn't come here to find a husband. I wanted to fulfill my father's dream. This place, these people, they need law and order."

"They need relief too," Joe told her. "What are you going to do about the high taxes?"

She frowned. "High taxes?"

"Law and order costs money," he tossed back at her. "The sheriff and Chase collect twenty percent off the top from every business except for Tom. He saves five percent for being mayor."

"That's robbery . . . extortion! It's criminal to charge such a high rate!"

"I'm supposed to be a judge," Joe said. "What can *we* do about it?"

"There has to be a complaint. Someone needs to file charges of Misuse of Public Funds or the like. Once a valid charge is leveled by a responsible citizen, the bookkeeping records for the town's expenses and payroll would have to be examined by an outside auditor."

"And who would protect the responsible citizen who dared make such a complaint against the most powerful crooks in the country?"

"There are always risks involved when it comes to seeking justice," Raylene replied.

"I think I know an easier route."

"What's that?"

Joe took a deep breath. "We have an election and pick a new man to run for sheriff. Pike Unger and his deputies are the leverage the Estcott brothers are using to fleece the people. Eliminate the sheriff, and we can set the new rules."

Raylene looked at him as if he had suddenly flipped upside down and was doing a handstand. "Joe, you're talking about starting a war. No one is going to run against Pike. He has too much control. With the Estcott brothers backing him, he can raise an army of gunmen to prevent an election."

"I can handle that end of things," Joe replied. "If this town had an honest judge and an honest sheriff, I'll bet we could cut those taxes in half. It would give all of these people up here a better life."

Raylene suddenly appeared frightened. "Father was never involved in anything like that. What if Pike fights back? What if he sends his men after us?"

Joe avoided her questions. "I did a little reading in those books you gave me and also did some asking around. Sheriff Unger is considered a county sheriff 'cause he oversees the mines and the nearby ranches too. A city marshal or city sheriff is usually appointed by a mayor or group of citizens. But a sheriff who rules over the entire county — he can be voted out of office."

"You're talking about getting involved in something that could get people killed. I'm not sure I want to be a part of it."

"Being a judge has made me see things more clearly," Joe told her truthfully. "I look around, and I see the people working long hours and still ending up near starving. I see the honest businesses about to go broke simply from trying to earn a living. And I want to do whatever it takes to make things better."

"Joe, you can't change the world all by yourself. A judge has no authority to make laws. It's your job to rule on the laws already in place."

"You just said there was likely crooked spending going on concerning these taxes."

"But it isn't up to you to put forward the investigation. You're a brand-new judge, not a resident citizen of this community."

"Maybe your calling ain't meant to be doing your father's work," Joe suggested, unhappy that she didn't understand what he was trying to do. "Maybe you're meant to start your own life and settle down with a man before you grow into an old spinster."

"Spinster!" Raylene flared. "I'm hardly approaching the age of becoming an old maid!"

Joe held his ground. "I reckon you know what I mean."

"My father devoted his life to trying to bring organized justice to this part of the country," Raylene ranted. "It was his dream, his purpose in life. I grew up standing at his side and being a part of his work."

"Yeah, but it was *his* work, not your own."

Joe could see he had said the wrong thing. A dark cloud rushed to color Raylene's complexion.

"I don't know why I bother to explain things to you," she practically hissed. "I shouldn't expect a law-dodging gambler to understand the value of my father's teachings."

Joe disliked the inflection of her voice and the implication of her words. "You'll have to forgive my ignorance, ma'am," he returned frigidly. "I sometimes forget that people like me are the reason men like your father wanted to set up shop in one of these forsaken towns. With some of us being such low-down and ignorant souls, I'm surprised anyone takes the time to concern him or herself with bringing us law and order."

The defiance and anger fled from Raylene's expression. "I didn't mean to put it in such a brutal way."

"You don't have to sugar-sweeten the truth," Joe said irritably. "Some of us uncouth sorts probably don't deserve nothing more than scorn from a proper lady such as yourself."

Raylene didn't have a response, so Joe turned aside and made for the rear exit. He half expected her to stop him and give him another lecture, but she did not.

Joe went through the back door and into the night. He paused after closing the door to allow his eyes to become accustomed to the gloom. Next, he took a quick look around. It wouldn't pay to get too careless. He saw nothing moving and assumed it was safe. Then a harsh whisper came out of the darkness.

"Howdy, Joe Bratt. Prepare to die."

CHAPTER NINE

Joe froze in position except to rotate his head enough to see a phantomlike figure standing at the corner of the building.

"You're him. I know you are." The man's voice sounded again, cold, sinister, and confident. "You spend most nights at the gambling table, while you pretend to be a judge."

"I don't know what you're talking about," Joe lied.

The man was a dark shadow some twenty-five feet away. "You're the one who killed Conroy Masterson's boy."

Joe slowly turned his body. Making no sudden movement, he nonetheless kept his hand several inches from his gun. He couldn't make out the dark figure's features, but he could see the pistol in the man's hand. To grab for his own weapon was to die.

"Who are you?" he asked, trying to gain

some time.

"A name belongs on a headstone, Bratt. I'm thinking you ought to have ordered a marker for yourself."

"I don't know who you think I am, but . . ."

"Let's not play silly games, Bratt," the shadow sneered. "I know you're the man I want . . . and it's time for you to pay your respects to the devil."

Joe searched his brain for a way to stop the man from simply killing him, but he drew a blank. He was facing the phantom now, but that only gave the man an easier target. Being so close, the fellow couldn't miss.

The door opened suddenly, and Raylene appeared at the entrance.

"Joe, I —" she began.

Surprised by the intrusion, the shadow swung his gun toward her, not knowing who might pop out of the building. It was the only chance Joe had, and he took it.

He yanked and fired his gun in an instant — once, twice, three times — all at the nearby phantom.

Raylene screamed in alarm, while the shadowy figure staggered backward. He managed to pull the trigger on his own gun, but the bullet whistled past Joe's head and slapped into the back railing of the wagon. Unable to manage a second shot, the man slowly doubled over and sprawled onto his face.

"Joe!" Raylene gasped, framed in the doorway, utterly stunned. "What on earth . . . ?"

But Joe kept his gun trained on the downed attacker. He moved cautiously forward until he could make out the dim outline of the man's body. The gun was lying next to his lifeless fingers. He knelt down and checked for a pulse, but his three shots had done the job. The man was dead.

"Bounty hunter or killer for hire," Joe finally said to Raylene. "He called me by my real name."

"He . . ." Raylene struggled to keep her voice under control. "He was going to kill you?"

"Sure as you're standing there," Joe replied. "If you hadn't opened the door when you did, I'd be in his place right now."

"I . . ." Raylene backed into the wall of the building and leaned heavily against it. One hand moved up to her brow, and she rotated her head back and forth. "You mean . . . I caused the death of . . ."

"You saved my life," Joe corrected, hurrying over to take hold of her arms and steady her. "He had me under his gun and was ready to shoot. He told me he had come to kill me."

Her eyes were wide, an incredulous expression on her face. "But why?"

"I would wager Conroy Masterson sent him. He's the father of the man I had to shoot in Pueblo."

There came curious shouts from the street and the sound of men running. Within a few moments several men had come around to the back of the church. Bulldog Vern was among them. Joe met the anxious crowd with a calm he didn't feel.

"He mistook me for someone else," Joe told the men. Then he explained how Raylene had opened the door just in time to save him from certain death.

"Hey!" one of the men exclaimed. "I know this jasper. He's a bounty killer from over Kansas way. Seen him bring in a body one time. His name is Taggart."

"Taggart!" Vern exclaimed. "I hear tell he's killed over a dozen men."

"Sure, I know about him — Bring-'em-in-Dead Taggart," put in another, leaning over the body to get a better look. "That's what everyone called him."

"You're one lucky son, Judge," the nearest man said to Joe. "This here is a man who

189

didn't miss what he aimed at."

"It's thanks to my sister that I got off the first shot," Joe replied. "Hit him square enough that he missed me." He stepped over and put a finger to the hole in the tailgate of the wagon. "But he sure 'nuff plugged my bedroom square."

"Don't reckon we need to have us a tribunal for the judge on this one, eh, boys?" one of the men said. "Plain as day self-defense."

"Couldn't call it nothing else," Vern agreed. "Everybody knows Taggart was a dirty, back-shooting killer." Then, with a glance at Joe, he added, "And the judge here ain't the sort to shoot down a man in cold blood."

Joe felt a wave of relief. With Bulldog Vern supporting him, no one would dare question his account of the shooting.

"Yup, the judge were mighty lucky," one of the crowd declared. "That Taggart, he were a bad one."

"One of you men, grab his feet, and we'll get him over to the carpenter's place," Vern instructed, taking over the scene. "Come daylight, we'll stuff this jasper into a box and give him a good-riddance burial."

"Thanks, Vern," Joe said. "And I thank all of you fellows for believing the truth of what happened here tonight."

Within a few minutes the body of the bounty hunter had been carted off. Joe took Raylene inside, sat her down on one of the stools, and poured her a tiny taste of liquor. He told her it would help to calm her nerves.

She took one sip and about strangled on it. "Ye gads!" she sputtered. "That's the worst stuff I ever put into my mouth. It tastes like fermented vinegar! How can you stand to drink something so disgusting?"

"It does take some getting used to."

She put the glass down onto the table and shoved it away. "I won't live long enough to ever get used to that."

Joe changed the subject. "Looks like you saved my life a second time."

Raylene grew sober once more. "My actions got a man killed."

"It was him or me," Joe reminded her. "If you had opened the door a split second later, I'd be the one being fitted for a box about now."

Raylene looked down at her trembling hands. "I can't stop shaking."

"Why don't you go to bed and —"

A knock at the back door stopped him in midsentence. Joe took a step in that direction, but the door was pushed open, and a hard-looking man filled the entrance. With dark hair and eyes, he wore denim pants and a leather vest over a cotton work shirt. His flat-crowned hat looked new and had a silver band. He eyed them both with unveiled suspicion as he took a step into the room.

"With you being a judge, I figured someone of position ought to run through your side of the story about this here killing." He explained his purpose. Then, puffing out his chest importantly, he announced, "I'm Chase Estcott, and I'm the one who oversees the sheriff and anything else that happens on the streets of Gold Butte."

"Pure case of mistaken identity, Mr. Estcott," Joe told him. "Taggart was looking to kill a man named Joe something."

Chase scowled at him. "Yeah, Bulldog told me your version of the fight. I checked Taggart's body and found a paper in his pocket — had the name Joe Bratt written on it. There was a description jotted down." He took a moment to scrutinize Joe. "You fit the bill, Judge — same weight, height, and hair coloring, and you like to gamble. Easy to see why he figured you were this Bratt character."

"Me or a hundred others, Estcott," he replied easily. "Fact is, you fit the description as well as me. I've heard you're quite a gambler too."

"He didn't draw down on me, Judge." Chase dismissed the argument. "Why did he pick you?"

"The guy said we arrived in town a day or two after the posse lost track of that Bratt fellow somewhere back in the hills." Joe filled in his own blanks. "I tried to tell him who I was, but he was set to kill me anyway. Before he could pull the trigger, Raylene opened the door, and he turned his gun on her. It gave me a chance to draw and fire first. I was lucky to hit him before he could swing the gun back on me."

"So your story goes," Chase commented cynically. "I'm supposed to believe this guy walked up and accused you of being this Joe Bratt fellow? Then he was going to shoot you down in cold blood, without knowing for certain if he even had the right man?"

"You said it yourself — I fit the description he needed," Joe said.

Chase glared at Raylene and then back at Joe. "I don't believe a word of what you're saying, Judge." He extended an arm and pointed a finger at Joe. "And I'll tell you another thing, mister. I aim to find out the truth. I think you're a lot more than you claim."

"Oh, yeah?" Joe showed his poker expression. "And what do you think I am, Est-cott?"

"Trouble!" he sneered, "with a capital *T!*"

Joe met his nasty gaze without wincing, feigning an innocence that would have made an angel blush. "I only came to Gold Butte to hand out justice to the wicked or them that choose an unlawful path, Chase. If you're among those who break the law, you'd best be starting to make things right."

Chase snorted his contempt. "I'll be watching you, Judge. You can count on it."

Joe didn't offer to speak again, and the man whirled about and stomped out of the room.

When the door slammed shut, Raylene ran to peek out and make sure the man had left.

"This is all my fault," she whispered harshly. "My bright idea got you into this, and now I've gotten a man killed. It's my doing! We should pack up and leave . . . right this minute!"

"Ease up on the reins, ma'am," Joe told her softly. "We've got a pile of chips in this here pot, and it's a mite early to fold."

Raylene spun on him like a tigress primed to pounce. "This isn't a game of cards!" she seethed. "Don't you understand? We killed a man tonight — you and me!"

"He was a low-life murderer, ma'am. Ain't

194

no one going to miss him none."

"He was a human being!"

"I doubt you could get odds on that at any gambling house."

Raylene threw her hands into the air and uttered an oath. "You're hopeless!" she cried. "Completely and utterly hopeless!"

Joe could see that the situation was growing worse by the second. Rather than try to calm Raylene or attempt to defuse her explosive temper, he lifted a hand, said, "Good night, ma'am," and made a hasty exit out to the wagon.

Joe climbed up onto his bed, kicked off his boots, set aside his hat, and pulled the blanket to cover him from the shoulders down. He lay there for a time trying to sort things out. It didn't matter to Raylene that Taggart had been a murderer, and, being honest with himself, it made little difference to the way he felt. He hadn't wanted to take another man's life, but he'd been given no more choice with Taggart than he had with Masterson. He was thankful to have survived both gunfights unscathed. However, the death of the bounty hunter brought with it a new concern. If Taggart had figured out who Joe was, how long would it be before someone else latched on to the same train of thought . . . especially now that the seed had been planted?

Time might be running out. Joe had to put his plan into action as soon as possible.

Raylene had trouble sleeping as well. She suffered a sizable dose of guilt. In her mind's eye, she kept replaying the deadly gunfight. If Taggart had not recognized her as a woman or thought she posed a threat, he would have killed her. Only his minute hesitation had allowed Joe to draw and kill him. She had overheard men in the crowd say that Taggart was a cold-blooded killer. There was no reason to mourn his passing. But she did. A life had been snuffed out that night, and she had helped to end that life.

Reflecting on the events that had led up to Taggart's death, she realized she had been purposely cruel to Joe. She had belittled him, and he had stomped out on her, angry and hurt by her attack. The instant he went out the door, reason forced her to go after him to apologize. The compelling desire to make up with him had saved his life.

Thinking about her attack on Joe caused her to toss her head back and forth. What was wrong with her? Why had she felt the need to strike out at him? Could it be that she resented the way he had taken his duties as a judge so seriously?

Following through with bringing a court of law to Gold Butte had been her idea, a tribute to her father's memory. She had wanted to feel the warmth and satisfaction of doing something good with her own life. However, Joe had handled the first case with a sense of justice beyond what the law books or her father had taught her. And Joe had taken it upon himself to hire work done on the courthouse and had even paid for it out of his own pocket. Joe knew nothing of being a judge, yet he had reached out and touched many of the people in Gold Butte. Lastly, he wanted to bring about change in the town, a change for the betterment of all of the people. Perhaps she was jealous of him for taking the initiative and exceeding what even her father would have done. He had usurped her dream and expanded its breadth. What if she secretly resented his ambition and success?

Have I become so petty?

She struggled to find answers to both her questions and her feelings. Another notion tugged at her consciousness, something she had fought to keep from entering her mind. What if she was developing a tender attachment to Joe? Perhaps her good sense was forcing her to alienate him for fear of . . .

what? A romantic relationship?

She immediately dismissed the idea.

Raylene! she scolded herself. *That's the dumbest notion you've ever had! What could you possibly have in common with a wandering gambler?*

But she could not deny the occasional flutter of her heart when they were together. She liked Joe, and, in spite of his lack of a proper education and his flippant manner, she admired him. Judicially challenged or not, he had a natural goodness that always seemed to shine through.

On a personal level he treated her with the utmost respect, but she had seen a faraway look in his eyes on occasion, as if he was daydreaming about her. And each time the subject of a suitor came up, it had definitely upset him. Somehow she didn't believe it was from worry for his own safety or of being discovered as a fraud. And if not, what did that leave?

If Joe did want their relationship to be more than that of business partners, why had he not acted on it? He had yet to make any kind of overture, not even trying to hold her hand. He kept his emotions intact and did each job as she outlined it for him. Maybe she was seeing something that wasn't there.

Turning to other matters, Raylene worried about what she was doing. The desire to realize her father's dream and her own personal ambition had taken over her life. Was this masquerade really for the good of the people of Gold Butte? Were her efforts directed only at providing them with a real court and a measure of justice? Or was she more interested in satisfying her own desire to judge from the bench and fill her father's shoes?

She hated the agitation within her chest. If her motives were truly selfish, it might negate all of the good she and Joe could do for these people. With so many notions floating about in her brain, it was going to be a long, fitful night.

Chase entered the Grub House and spied Dunn at his usual table for breakfast. He sauntered over, pulled out a second chair, and slumped down with a disgusted grunt.

"That chore is finished," he opened the conversation.

Dunn placed his fork next to a near-empty plate and pushed back from the table. "What are you talking about?"

"We planted Taggart's body early this morning," Chase began. "No one bothered to say a prayer for his soul."

"I doubt any amount of prayer would alter his destination in the Hereafter," Dunn said.

"Do you believe the story about mistaken identity?" Chase asked.

Dunn shrugged. "Regardless of whether Stanfield is who he claims to be or not, it sounds like it was a kill-or-be-killed situation."

"Bulldog was one of the first to arrive. He believes it happened like the judge said."

"If Vern vouches for him, I'd say that closes the book on Taggart."

"On Taggart maybe, but I don't know about the judge. I've been doing some checking on him" — Chase narrowed his gaze — "on my own."

"Oh?" Dunn hid his displeasure over his brother's going behind his back. "And what did you find out about our mystery man?"

"I talked to a stagecoach driver this morning, the one who takes the Denver run. He knew a little about Judge Gordon Stanfield." Chase showed a smirk. "It seems Stanfield was a circuit judge over at Sunset on occasion."

"Go on," Dunn encouraged.

Smugly, he added, "The driver said Judge Stanfield always had his grown daughter with him." He waited for Dunn to speak, but his brother didn't offer any comment.

"Anyway, Stanfield and his girl traveled the country together all the while he was riding as a circuit judge." He drew his eyebrows together. "The driver says he heard a rumor about how the judge wanted to find a town where he and his daughter could set up shop in a permanent way."

Dunn lifted a shoulder in a careless shrug. "So the old boy was a circuit judge, traveling with his daughter. So what?"

"The daughter's name was Raylene. At least we know she's the right gal. The old judge was Gordon Stanfield."

"I don't know where this is going, Chase. We know the judge is the junior and his father was the senior, and he readily admits he took over when his father died."

Chase snickered. "Yeah, only the old whip from the stage says Gordon didn't have a son. Everyone knew about the girl, but nary a soul ever heard about any boy in the family."

Dunn thoughtfully rubbed his chin. "The boy could have left home at an early age. Perhaps he and his father were estranged for some reason."

"And he just happened to show up when the old man died in a wagon mishap?"

"You think he's an impostor." It was a statement.

"That'd be my guess, big brother," Chase confirmed. "Maybe he is the man Taggart was after."

Dunn did not hide his skepticism. "Of course, most wanted men hide from the law by becoming a judge."

"His false identity could be a cover for another motive. The man could be a union organizer."

"Except he hasn't made any attempt to gather information from or to speak to the miners in private. I have enough eyes and ears working for me, we'd have learned about any secret meetings."

"Vern said he had a couple of the miners' wives and kids working for him. They cleaned up the courtroom and upholstered the benches for him."

"That hardly constitutes organizing a union."

"Why else would a man come here pretending to be something he isn't?" Chase asked. "I say he's got to be one of them union sorts. We both know they're attempting to unionize miners all over the country."

"So far, his 'plan' has only been to hand out a very appropriate sentence to Victor Boggs and to fix up the old barn and make it look more like a courthouse inside. He's even managed to win over Bulldog Vern and

Keno — and they both tried to run him out of town!"

"All right, so he's a sneaky sort," Chase argued. "He might be waiting till we aren't expecting anything. Either that, or he could be here for something else altogether."

Dunn considered the possibilities. "I don't know what that could be. So far he has done nothing but act like a judge."

"Something is up with this guy, Dunn," Chase said thickly, "and I think we ought to find out what."

"I don't want to cause a stink around town. I allowed you to run the other two judges off without a lot of backlash, but they both had reputations as being union supporters. They could have done a lot of damage to the harmony we have here in Gold Butte. This new judge actually spends his evenings at the casino gambling. If he isn't out to harm our businesses, there's certainly no need to run him off." Dunn snorted. "Besides which, I don't think he's the kind of man who would run."

"I 'spect he proved he was up for a fight when Bulldog and Keno went to visit," Chase agreed. "And he put Taggart into his final resting place in short order. I'm for thinking that's all the more reason we ought to get to the bottom of this here mystery.

He's proved he's a dangerous man."

"We'll continue to do this my way, Chase." Dunn concluded the discussion.

"You don't fool me." Chase grated out the words. "You're only worried about what your gemstone of a wife will say. Ever since you married her, you've become a milksop, a weak-kneed mama's boy — and she's your new mother!"

Dunn slammed a clenched fist onto the tabletop hard enough that several heads turned in their direction. However, instead of raising his voice, he calmly returned the curious stares until people went back to their own business. Then he spoke to his brother in a hushed, firm voice.

"I'm growing weary of your making Myra the butt of your excuses and arguments, Chase. She is the best thing ever to come into my life. I won't have you speaking ill of her or blaming her for everything that goes wrong in this town. From now on, you keep a civil tongue whenever you mention her." He leaned forward and glared hard at his younger brother. "Do I make myself clear?"

"You're the boss," Chase acquiesced, but the bitterness and defiance remained in his gaze. "I'll be around if you need me."

Dunn watched as his brother rose and swaggered out of the cafe. He was like an ambitious dust devil, circling about, trying to suck up debris and enough gale force to grow into a tornado. One day soon the two of them were going to tangle horns.

CHAPTER TEN

It had been an uneventful week since the death of the bounty hunter named Taggart. Joe had sent a wire to Pueblo informing the authorities of his death along with the circumstances. He received word back, and Tom had kept the news quiet. Everything was starting to fall into place.

"Good morning, ma'am," Joe greeted Raylene. "Thought I smelled breakfast cooking."

Raylene showed him a scowl. "Are you ever going to stop calling me *ma'am?*" she declared. "Someone is going to overhear you."

"I keep telling you, I ain't never been on a first-name basis with a decent woman. It don't come natural."

"If I could impress two things upon you, Joe, it would be to stop using the word *ain't* and calling me *ma'am!*"

Joe ducked his head. "It ain . . ." — he

caught himself — "isn't that easy."

Raylene turned the eggs, knowing Joe liked his cooked throughout, then asked, "What's the real problem, Joe? Why is it so hard to use my name?"

Joe gave a shake of his head and lifted his eyes to gaze at her. "Because I'm not worth the ground you walk on . . . and we both know it."

The conviction of his words appeared to shock Raylene.

"That isn't true," she debated at once. "Each man's worth is decided by what he accomplishes with his life. You don't have to be rich or famous to be a special person. You needn't be a great doctor or scientist. Any man can attain a measure of decency and honor by having a good heart and trying to help others."

"What about a gambler who's killed two men; a man who goes around pretending to be a judge?" he challenged.

"You had no choice in either of those deaths, and it was my idea to pass you off as my brother and a judge. If there is blame or dishonor in what we have done, it's on my head, not yours. Personally, I think you've made a good showing up to this point."

Joe gave that a moment's thought, while

Raylene dished up portions of eggs and ham onto two plates. She proceeded to pour two cups of coffee and then sat down.

"I commence to see why you would make a good lawyer, ma'am," he told her, taking his place across the table from her. When she took a bite, rather than responding to his using the word *ma'am* again, he changed the subject.

"I've been doing some thinking about this here job, and I've decided we have to help the people of Gold Butte," Joe said.

"Help them?"

"These here folks stood up for me when I had to kill Taggart, took me at my word without your even telling your side of the story. I've met a fair number of good men here in town, and I think we ought to go ahead with the election."

"Who would dare run against Sheriff Unger?" she asked.

"I've got just the guy for the job, but I want your go-ahead."

"Let me think on it for a day or two, Joe. There's something else I need to tell you." She seemed hesitant to speak, then blurted it out. "I have an outing tomorrow."

Joe waited with a poker face, hiding the immediate knot that twisted within his stomach.

"Tom's brother," she continued, "Pete Lawson, asked me to go for a ride. He runs the express office and does some work with Tom."

"I've seen him around," Joe said, displaying no outward emotion. "He sharpens the drill bits and chisels for the miners. It's cheaper to have him put a new edge on a drill than it is to buy a new one."

"Yes, I know what he does," she said. "We're going on a picnic, and he intends to show me some caves where there are some markings from an ancient civilization. It's quite a long way, but we expect to be back before dark."

"Whatever you want to do is fine with me. It ain't like you have to check with me first." Joe's voice was under control, but the words came out frigid.

"I can't say no to everyone, Joe," Raylene attempted to explain. "If I did, it might cause questions about us . . . about whether we are actually brother and sister."

Joe took a bite of food, but it had no flavor. Either that or it was completely diluted by the bitterness of knowing that Raylene would again be cavorting with some man.

"Remember, our subterfuge is for a good cause." Raylene continued to seek his understanding.

"You mean it's for *your* cause."

Raylene took exception to his statement. "Joe, I chose to accompany Pete because he's a gentleman, and —"

"I told you, it don't matter!" Joe barked at her. "You don't have to explain nothing to me! I know you're the most popular thing to hit this town since the invention of ice cream. Do whatever you've a mind to. You don't need my approval."

"You need to know where I'm at . . . in case something should come up."

"I'm a gambler, remember?" He shot the words at her. "I know how to bluff and when to fold. I won't ruin this setup for you. I promised you three months, and I'll darn well give you them three months." Then he rose from the table, his food barely touched, whirled around, and headed back through the living quarters.

Raylene wanted to shout at him to stop, but she did not. He was upset and would need time to deal with his anger. She knew he disliked being trapped in a lie, but this outburst was more on a personal level. His behavior certainly resembled jealousy.

She dismissed the quandary for the moment. She needed to clean up the dishes and start work on a couple of rulings Joe was going to make. His decisions would earn needed fees to pay expenses to keep their — well, *her* — courthouse open. She had to remain focused on the reason they were here. She owed whatever justice she could provide to her father's memory. She dearly wanted to believe he would have been proud of her.

Chase had seen Myra walk down the street and enter the mercantile. That was a chore he would never tire of — watching Myra. He remained unobtrusive, picking out a place where he could keep an eye on Lawson's place. He found a shady spot and hunkered down. Next, he rolled and lit himself a cigarette, idly smoking and sitting on his heels, waiting for Myra to reappear. Resting there, he felt a gloom settle over his shoulders. Nothing between himself and his brother had been the same since Myra entered Dunn's life. She had formed a wedge between them, changing his brother into a different man. Business, wealth, power — that had been Dunn's life before her. But now he had become weak, a fawning puppy, seeking to be a respected pillar of society. Everything had changed. Chase had been his point man, the one who led the charge, a leader of tough, hard men.

Now he had become Dunn's lackey, a lame hired hand, little more than a town runner for his big brother.

Chase silently cursed the day Myra had come into their lives. She was young, charming, with a beauty beyond compare. Why choose a man with such an age difference? She should have been looking for someone like himself. He was nine years younger than Dunn, filled with a youth and energy that would have provided for her every need. He would have been a much better match for her. He knew that once she belonged to him, she would have felt fortunate and proud to have a man like him on her arm. Instead, a good many people thought of her as a gold digger, a prize doll, a pretty baby for the rich and powerful Dunn Estcott. She was nothing more than a trophy for him, something to show off and pretend he still had thirty good years left in him. It was a dirty, rotten shame, that's what it was.

When Myra finally reappeared, the wisp of a smile was on her face, and she carried a single package under one arm. Something new had probably come in from back east, another trinket to clog her overstuffed closets.

Chase leered after her with a gnawing

hunger in his gut. The breeze stirred her skirt as she stepped down from the wooden walkway. The combination exposed her ankles and caused the skirt to cling to the outline of her trim legs. Chase swallowed the immediate rise of passion but could not slow the racing of his heart.

She should be my woman, he thought bitterly. *Durned if I don't deserve Myra more than Dunn!*

The next day was not much fun for Joe. He ate a silent breakfast with Raylene and then went to work on the spare room. He had the partition in place and had built a box frame for a straw mattress. It would only take another day or two of hard work, and it would be finished.

Pete showed up to collect Raylene at midmorning. She had donned her best outfit for their jaunt into the country, a dark gray-and-blue, long-sleeved dress with a white sun bonnet. Once aboard his carriage, she smiled and waved good-bye to Joe. He lifted a hand in return, but envy tore a hole in his gut at the idea of her spending a whole day being wooed by another man.

Joe busied himself with chores to occupy his mind. When he grew tired, he went to the kitchen and removed a worn deck of cards from his jacket pocket. He was playing a game of solitaire at the kitchen table, when a melodic voice called out from the meeting room.

"Yoo-hoo! Judge!" It was a woman's voice. "Are you here?"

Joe left the table, went through the door, and spied Myra Estcott. She stood inside the courtroom entrance with her hands locked behind her back.

"Oh, there you are!" she said, flashing a winsome smile.

"Mrs. Estcott," he greeted her, "what brings you here today?"

Myra came forward and produced a slip of paper, holding it out for him. "I thought these might be something you could use," she chirped giddily, "you know, to make the courtroom more official."

Joe took the slip of paper and discovered it was a receipt. It listed *one office desk* and *two chairs,* with an amount of thirty-six dollars listed at the bottom. Next to the amount were the words *PAID IN FULL.*

"For the courthouse?" He was incredulous. "You bought a desk and chairs for us?"

She continued to smile. "For the town," she corrected. "I had Tom order the set for you, and they arrived with yesterday's delivery. He said he'll help you move the furniture here whenever you like."

"I wish my sister was here," he said, feeling a rush of emotion. "She's much better at saying a proper thanks than me. I . . . I'm . . . I'm durn thankful, Mrs. Estcott. Guess there isn't another term to express my feelings."

She uttered another girlish laugh. "Well, you have been settling disputes for the past couple of weeks, and it didn't seem right, your having to stand up and use an old minister's pulpit while making your rulings or doing your decision-making."

"This is a mighty . . ." Thinking of some of the words he had learned, he concluded, "This is a mighty fine civic-duty kind of thing to do, ma'am. Makes me feel all humble inside."

"I heard about how you helped out one of the miner's family by hiring them," she admitted. With a quick look around, she said, "And it is a wonderful improvement. But a judge shouldn't have to pay for his own courthouse. That is something the town should provide."

"I truly admire your thinking, Mrs. Estcott."

Myra laughed again. "I so enjoy the candid way you talk, Judge. You are so very much an average man."

"And that's a good thing, huh?"

The lady turned serious. "My folks had a circle of friends made up of elected officials, judges, doctors — the most socially elite for a hundred miles around. The judges I met were good men, but they were similar to my college professors at Vassar. I found them to be pious and knowledgeable but also lofty and intimidating. I never would have felt comfortable going to any of them with a personal problem, because I was afraid they would think poorly of me." She shrugged. "I suppose part of the reason is because I was quite young, and they were men of position and prominence."

"And I don't strike you that way?"

She again smiled at him. "You don't espouse a know-it-all attitude or demonstrate the pretense of scholarly authority. You come across more like a friend or neighbor dispensing advice. I don't feel ill-at-ease or threatened when I'm around you."

"I'm glad I don't make you skittish, ma'am. I reckon it's important that people can come to their town judge when they have an issue he might be able to help with. I don't claim to have all the right answers, but I sure am willing to listen carefully and give it my best shot."

"I believe you are an insightful man," Myra said, lowering her head. "Being such, you undoubtedly have an opinion as to why Dunn and I are a couple."

"People get married for a number of reasons." Joe kept his voice nonjudgmental. "If you take your wedding vows seriously and are happy with your choice, no one ought to fault your being together."

"I am a faithful wife," she said quickly. "I would never do anything to hurt Dunn."

"In my book, that makes you a good woman."

"And Dunn treats me special and does absolutely everything he can to make me happy."

"Sounds like a good marriage to me."

Myra gazed at him, displaying a sheepish look. "I never got a blessing from my parents. Father is a bank president and a member of the town council. He spent a lot of money to send me back east for schooling. I know my folks had dreams for me — a future as an educated woman, perhaps a teacher or administrator of some kind. By marrying Dunn, I fear I let them down."

"Parents should always try to do what is best for their children," Joe surmised, "but it don't always match up with what the children want out of life. You seem a good person and devoted wife, Mrs. Estcott. I figure, if your folks knew you really loved Dunn and could see that you are happy and content, they would be proud of you."

"I don't know." Myra was not convinced. "They expected me to use my education, and they wanted grandchildren from me." A light suddenly came into her eyes. "I quit school to marry Dunn, and we have not yet been blessed with any children."

Joe could read most people's faces when they drew the card they wanted. "You're still young," he said, keeping his notion to himself.

Myra smiled. "Yes, that's true." When he added nothing more, she said, "Dunn mentioned that you often play cards at night. He said that if you lost your job as a judge, he would certainly hire you to work in his casino."

Joe laughed, but he was curious. "How does your family feel now, with you so far away and all? Do you keep in touch?"

The smile faded. "I wish we were on speaking terms, but . . . well, as I told you, they were very disappointed in me."

"They've had time to think it over and accept your decision," Joe said. "I'd wager they still love and miss you."

Strangely, Myra's eyes filled with tears.

"Do you really think so?"

"I can't imagine any parent not being proud of a lady like you, Mrs. Estcott. You could have been a money-grubbing snoot, but you're not. You've told me how much you love your husband, and you've spent your time and money to make a difference by sprucing up our courtroom. That tells me you are a caring and decent person."

She sniffed back her tears. "Thank you for the kind words, Judge."

"Does your family even know where you are?"

"I haven't spoken to or written to them since the wedding. I didn't think they would want to hear from me."

"I don't figure parents were meant to love their kids only when they do the things they want them to. They can't stop being your parents. Why not write them a letter and tell them how this marriage to Dunn is working out? Let them know you're happy with the choice you made. If a baby should come along one day, they will certainly want to get to know their own grandchild. I'll lay you three-to-one they answer right back."

Myra's face lit up. "I'm going to do it!" she declared. "I'll tell them all about the lovely trips we take to Denver, about how Dunn is so sweet and considerate. I'll make them understand that I made the right decision by marrying him."

"Sounds like a fine idea, ma'am."

She was visibly excited. "Thank you, Judge!" She took a step toward the door and stopped. "Oh, I hope you enjoy the desk and chairs."

"It's going to be a real improvement, and I thank you again, Mrs. Estcott."

Myra practically scampered from the meeting house, eager to write and send off a letter to her folks.

Joe wished he knew their address. He would have sent a letter to them as well, telling them what a wonderful young lady their girl had become.

CHAPTER ELEVEN

It was a freak accident. Pete and Raylene had left the horse tied off to a cedar tree while they walked up and inspected the old ruins. The mare had been standing quietly when they left. However, a snake or something had given the horse a start. When she spooked, she stepped backward and hooked her back leg over the singletree. Becoming excited, she had tried to kick loose of the tangle, lost her balance, and fell down. Then, trapped in the harness, panicked to get back onto her feet, she had kicked, twisted, and lunged until she ended up breaking her front leg.

With the horse unable to walk, Pete had been forced to end her misery. And now he and Raylene were stranded, no fewer than fifteen miles from the nearest house or ranch.

"It'll be dark in an hour or two," Raylene lamented their predicament. "How are we going to get back to town?"

"I'll walk it," Pete said. "You have the blanket we used for our picnic, and I'll round up some wood and start a fire. You can stay warm while I make the trip into town. I ought to make Gold Butte by morning. I'll rent a couple of horses at the livery and come back for you."

Raylene took a long look around. There were endless hills dotted with cedar trees and scrub brush. They were several miles off the main trail, with only a little water and a few leftovers from their picnic lunch.

"I don't want to wait here all night, Pete. My brother will be worried to death."

Pete gave a negative shake of his head. "I don't know what else we can do, Raylene. It will take me at least two or three hours to reach the main trail. By then it will be well past dark, so I don't expect to meet any travelers on the road."

"Then we'll walk back to town together. You said we could make it by morning."

"I said I could probably do it," he said, glancing down at her feet. "You're not exactly dressed to walk that far — especially without walking shoes."

Raylene vented her frustration in her reply. "I can darn well try."

■ ■ ■ ■

Joe became concerned when Raylene didn't show up before dark. Her usual time to go to bed came, and she still hadn't returned. However, she had warned him the trip was going to be a long one — old drawings at an Indian cave or some such thing. Raylene had said she might be home late and he should not worry.

Yeah, he thought, don't worry. She's only out there under the moonlight, probably snuggled up next to Pete Lawson. Being a proper gentleman, Tom's brother would likely slip his arm around her shoulders to help keep off the chill of the night air. He might even have stopped on a hill, where they could gaze at the rising moon, while he whispered sweet words into one of her charming, delicate ears. Why should he worry about that?

Joe, knowing his mind would be elsewhere, didn't feel like playing cards. He climbed into the back of the wagon and lay down on his bed. He made an attempt to quash any thoughts of Raylene, but it was wasted effort. He tossed and turned for an hour, then wondered if he should get up and check to see if she was home yet. He decided against it. He didn't want another lecture about intruding into her life or trying to be over-protective.

Joe pondered his idea about an election. Everything was set. He needed only to pick a date and make the announcement. After that, well . . . he would have to let the afterward take care of itself. He saw the struggling businessmen and the half-starved kids running around every day. He knew most of the miners' wives had not had a free dime to spend in months. This dire situation was something Raylene's father would have encountered and dealt with. He imagined a real judge would have had better ideas about how to fix things, but Joe had made his plan and figured it could work. It was the best he had to offer.

Now, with a chance to play a role he had not earned, he did have a notion of what the other side felt like. He recalled the joy and hope he had seen in the faces of Kate Miller and Marge when he paid them for their hard work. He considered Myra Est-cott, how she had taken it upon herself to provide a desk and chairs for the court-house. He recalled her bright, misty eyes when he had told her to write to her folks. He sure hoped they answered back and told her they loved her.

It felt good, trying to help other people with life's problems. It provided enough of a warm feeling that it almost offset the jealousy that plagued him about Raylene.

Joe arose the next morning and tended to the animals. He drew a pan of water from the pump and returned to the wagon. After a quick wash and shave, he entered the living quarters to see if Raylene was up yet.

"Ma'am?" He spoke up from the kitchen and looked expectantly at the bedroom door. "Are you awake?"

There was complete silence.

Joe walked over to knock but discovered the door was not fully closed. It gave way before his knuckles, and he could see the still-made bed. Raylene had not returned from her outing.

Like a cold gust of wind, there came an instant unsettling in Joe's stomach. A tightness gripped his chest, and a pang of fear bolted through him. Something had gone wrong. Something bad had happened to Raylene.

His first impulse was to dash out back, saddle up his horse, and go search for her. However, he didn't have any idea of where to look. Several possible scenarios flashed through his head. Maybe Pete had kidnapped Raylene for some reason. What if they had been attacked by rogue bandits or renegade Indians? Logically, Pete was not the likely sort to kidnap a woman. And there had been no trouble with the Indians since Gold Butte was founded. Lastly, those two would have had very little worth stealing for any bandits. The only conclusion was that something unforeseen had happened on their journey to or from the old caves. They'd likely had an accident and were broken down along the trail. Perhaps one of them was injured, and they could not get back to the wagon.

Without wasting more time on speculation, Joe exited the courthouse and headed down the street. Before he could reach the general store, he saw three cowboys stagger out of the saloon.

"Yee-hah!" the taller one of the three cried, and he fired his gun into the air.

"Say so long for two months!" yelled another. "Trail-drive time!" And he also fired his gun.

The barkeep appeared behind them with a club in his hand. "Hold on!" he shouted. "You boys owe for some damages!"

"Them two miners started it," claimed the third man, the only one with his gun still in its holster. "Make them pay!"

"It don't work that way, boys," the barkeep told them. "Every man pays his share, one by each."

The tall man spun about with his gun and pointed it at the barkeep. "You'd best back off, bartender, else you might be picking lead out of your teeth."

As the three men were all facing the bartender, Joe moved right out behind them and drew his gun.

"Stand easy, you three," he commanded. "Any one of you makes a twitch, and I'll blow a hole through your gullets."

Keno, aroused by the shooting, had come rushing down the street. He also pulled his gun and covered the three men.

"Do as the judge says, boys," Keno warned them. "You don't want to test the aim of the man who killed Bring-'em-in-Dead Taggart, the bounty hunter."

The news sobered the three men on the spot. They dropped their weapons without further protest.

"Listen to me, Judge," the one began to plead their case, "we've got to get back. The herd is gathered for the trail drive, and Mr. Lewis can't get them moving without us."

"You." Joe pointed his weapon at the only man who hadn't fired his gun. "How long will it take you to go get Mr. Lewis and bring him to town?"

"I 'spect it wouldn't take more'n a couple hours."

"Get moving then." As the man picked up his gun and headed for his horse, Joe added, "And tell him to bring his money pouch." Turning his attention to the remaining pair, he ordered, "Keno, put these other two men in a cell until Mr. Lewis arrives."

"You got it, Judge." Keno waved his gun. "Reckon you boys know the way. Let's go get comfy."

Once they had left, Joe approached the bartender. "Open kind of late, aren't you?"

"You know how it is, Judge. They wanted a last fling before heading out for two months on the trail. I don't blame them none for that. Mixing it up with the miners was more fun than a fight, but they sure enough busted the place up some."

"Give me the details, and show me the damages," Joe told him.

"Sure thing, Judge."

Joe hated to delay looking for Raylene. As soon as he had this situation in hand, he would have Tom ride out to see what had happened. Tom would know where to look and would find his brother quicker than Joe. He muttered a "Damn" under his breath and went into the saloon.

■ ■ ■ ■

Joe settled the damages and fine with the rancher and let his boys go with a stern warning not to come to town looking for quite so much excitement next time. They had barely left when Raylene appeared at the door.

"What was that all about?" she asked.

"Some boys from the Lewis ranch were whooping it up a little extra at the saloon and got to busting things up with a couple miners. They're starting a trail drive today and decided to let off a little steam their last night before pulling out."

"You didn't even miss me," she murmured softly. "I was afraid something would come up and you would need me. . . ." But she stopped speaking, as if choked with emotion.

"I only did like you've been teaching me."

"What about the new desk and chairs?" she asked, fixing her gaze on the new furniture.

"Myra Estcott bought those for the courthouse," Joe explained. "Tom and I moved them over after you went off gallivanting with Pete."

Joe stood patiently for a time and waited.

Raylene remained with her head lowered, as if she didn't have the strength to look up at him.

"Have you eaten breakfast?" he asked when she didn't offer to speak.

"I've just had the worst night of my life," Raylene admitted. "I'm too tired to even walk to my bed."

Joe didn't hesitate. He moved over, slipped one arm under Raylene's legs and the other around her shoulders. Then he lifted her up into his arms.

"No!" Raylene found strength for resistance. "Joe, don't!"

But Joe ignored her protest and carried her toward the living quarters. "I'll fix you something to eat, then I'll heat some water, and you can have a nice, relaxing bath."

"Joe, you don't have to . . ."

"After you soak for a spell" — he didn't let her continue — "you can get some sleep." Then he put a sharp stare on her. "Pete didn't get frisky with you or anything, did he?"

"Of course not," she was quick to respond. "The horse broke its leg, and we had to walk back from the old ruins. Tom arrived in time to give me a ride the last couple miles. He went back to get his brother and the carriage."

"Dad-gum!" Joe exclaimed, teasing. "Sure hate to think of you having so much fun with some guy other than me."

"What are you talking about?"

"You remember how I showed up shot and all, after you had lost the wheel from your wagon?" He continued the jest. "I wanted that to be a special memory. Now you go out and try to have a bigger adventure with some other guy."

Raylene didn't have a comment for that. Joe pushed past the bedroom door and gently placed Raylene down on her bed. Then he went to the kitchen and fried up some eggs, potatoes, and a couple thick strips of salt pork. He also heated up the coffee he had fixed for his own breakfast.

By the time he returned to the bedroom, Raylene had removed her dust-covered clothes and was clad in her sleeping gown. The material was quite worn and of a much lighter weight than her usual outfits. In fact, it was thin enough for Joe to take notice of the outline of her feminine features.

Joe averted his eyes like a gentleman and kept his mind on business, offering up the plate of food and a cup of coffee. Raylene took several sips of the coffee and then began to eat. She cleaned the plate in about five minutes flat. Her appetite was heartier than Joe had witnessed since he met her.

"That was very good, Joe," Raylene said, handing him the empty plate. "I guess the old saying is true: food tastes better when someone else does the cooking."

"I'll heat some water for your bath."

Raylene gave a shake of her head. "I'd rather get some sleep first. I'm too tired to enjoy a real bath."

"All right, ma'am," Joe told her. "You get some sleep, and don't fret about anything but taking it easy today."

She sighed wearily, *"Raylene,* not *ma'am."*

"Yeah, whatever you say." He didn't apologize. "You get some rest."

"Thank you, Joe," Raylene murmured, reclining on the bed as he backed out of her room. "Thank you for taking care of me."

"Yeah" was his final word before he closed the door and left her to rest.

"You bought the judge a desk?" Dunn was incredulous. "And two chairs too?"

"For the courthouse," Myra replied. "He and his sister certainly can't afford to fix the place up. I don't know how they afford food for their table."

Dunn rubbed his hands together. "I've told you how the man wins at poker most nights. I'll bet he earns more each week than a dozen miners combined."

"I wanted to do something nice for them," Myra insisted. "You know, kind of welcome them to the community."

"I understand," he said carefully. "But I hate to see you working so hard to keep the courthouse going, when the judge might up and close his doors in a week or two. You do remember the other two judges?"

"Yes, but they weren't like Judge Stanfield. He isn't going to desert us."

"I haven't said anything to you before, Myra honey, but the judge might not be exactly who and what he claims to be."

She gave him a curious frown. "What do you mean?"

"Chase has been doing some checking on him." The mention of his brother immediately altered Myra's frown into a dark scowl. "I didn't ask him to," he hastily assured her. "Anyway, he spoke to one of the stage drivers, a man who knew Raylene's father."

"Of course he did. And?" she asked, her voice as cool as a morning frost.

"From all the years the driver knew the old man, he never heard of Gordon Stanfield *junior*. It seems the son didn't exist until he and Raylene showed up in town."

"He explained that," Myra countered. "He admitted to having been a gambler before his father passed on. Raylene said he joined her at the last minute."

"What about the bounty hunter? The one he killed out back of the courthouse?"

"It was mistaken identity." She continued to defend him. "You don't really believe he's a killer, running from the law?"

Dunn raised both hands, hoping to put an end to this line of conversation. "I'm only trying to point out that the judge might not stick around."

Myra's mouth became a rigid line, while her neatly trimmed eyebrows drew tightly together. "The judge and Raylene haven't done one blessed thing to indicate they are here to do anything more than provide us with a courthouse and dispense law and order, Dunn."

"I agree, but Chase thinks the judge is up to no good. I suppose I can understand why he might have grounds for suspicion."

"Your brother is taking on a lot of responsibility for himself. I thought you were the one who gave the orders around here."

"He's only trying to protect our interests. If the judge was to help start up a union for the miners, it could ruin us."

Myra allowed the statement to go unchallenged. "Chase's suspicions aside, what is your take on Judge Stanfield?" she wanted to know. "Are you also going to try to prove he isn't who he claims?"

"It depends on what we find out about him and whether he's pretending to be something he's not."

Myra gave her head a negative toss. "I don't like it, Dunn. The judge might be a little unorthodox, but his goal seems very straightforward to me. Did you hear how he went out and captured those three rowdy cowboys single-handedly? Does a union organizer do that?"

"Myra honey, I'm not looking to find fault with the man. I hope he actually is an ex-gambler who became a judge. My concern is in relation to how much we don't know about him. What if he is here for a purpose we haven't determined yet?"

"He's been here several weeks, Dunn. Has he been down at the mines or organized any meetings?"

"No, but . . ."

"Well, everyone in town believes he's exactly what he says he is. As for Raylene, she is a very sweet young lady. I can't believe she would condone any deception that would undermine or discredit the memory of her father."

"If the judge is who he claims and has no ulterior motives, I'll be first in line to support him. That ought to be fair enough."

Myra uttered an unfeminine grunt. "Gadfry, Dunn!" she said bitterly. "I'd hate to be you. It must be terrible to be so suspicious of everyone."

Dunn wanted to reassure her, but Myra spun around and stormed out of the room. He'd made her angry, and that was never a good idea. Once her hackles were up, she would give him the silent treatment and look at him as if he had told a group of children there would be no Christmas that year. He resigned himself to being miserable until they made up.

Punching a fist into the palm of his other hand, he paced the room and steadfastly firmed his resolve. Whether Myra liked it or not, he had to know the truth about Judge Gordon Stanfield — if that was even the man's name. His wife had a trusting nature and took everyone at face value. He knew better. He was a businessman first and foremost. He had to trust his instincts.

Joe was trying to fit a door to his new bedroom when Raylene returned from shopping at the mercantile. She took the grocery items into the kitchen and returned to where he was working. He stopped at her approach and turned to face her.

"I ran into Myra Estcott at the store. She seems to have had a spat with Dunn about you. I hope she isn't going to be devastated when she learns the truth."

"I sure would hate to disappoint her," Joe replied. "Buying the courthouse a desk and chairs? That's something ordinary folks don't do every day."

Raylene had a serious expression on her recently sunburned face. "I envy you sometimes, Joe."

He was shocked by her statement. "Say what?"

"For having such easy communication with the people," Raylene explained. "My father was stern and a bit pompous, more like a ruler or dictator of the law, while you manage to come across like a friend giving advice."

"A man like your father commanded respect," Joe argued. "I don't have his good character or knowledge to fall back on. I can't be more than I am."

"I think you were destined to be more than a gambler. You work so well with people."

It suddenly felt very warm in the room. "Hardly that," he said. "I'm only trying to fulfill my debt to you."

"Joe." Raylene murmured his name and

gazed at him with an odd sort of look. Less alert or inquisitive, rather it was more dreamy, as if she was wistfully thinking of something nice. "You've never been anything but a perfect gentleman around me."

He wondered where that statement came from and what it could possibly mean. "You're a right proper lady," he rationalized.

"Yes, but I'm not unaware of your jealousy at the attention I receive from other men. It has been evident in your behavior and the way you treat me."

Joe shrugged off the conclusion. "A man ought to be protective of his sister."

"Is that what I am to you, Joe?" she asked, leaning a bit closer. "Do you think of me as your sister?"

Joe felt trapped — yet in a good way. The perfumed scent from Raylene's toilet water filled his nostrils, her body so close he could almost hear her heart beating. Her eyes were liquid pools, beckoning him to dive in and join her. He battled down the desire to take her into his arms. She was a proper lady, a judge's daughter, as pure and innocent as a spring sunrise. He didn't have the right to hold her hand, let alone indulge in romantic notions about her.

"I reckon you're about the most special

lady I ever met," Joe said after a short, internal war. "If I had ever had me a sister, I'd have been proud to have her be as wonderful as you."

The words were meant as flattery, but he didn't miss the instant change in Raylene's demeanor. The ardent, wistful look in her eyes was instantly replaced by a narrow scowl. Her shoulders drew back, and she came erect.

"I'm so glad I would have made a nice sister." The words were delivered in a harsh, cynical tone. "If you had been born my brother, I'm sure we'd have gotten along famously."

"Ma'am, I don't know —"

"And stop calling me *ma'am!*" she snapped, even more incensed. "Why can't you learn to call me by my first name? Is it so hard to remember?"

Joe surrendered to his runaway emotions and dismissed his good sense. "I call you *ma'am,*" he barked back, taking hold of her shoulders with both hands, "because" — he yanked her against his chest — "if I don't remind myself to think of you as *ma'am,* I might do something stupid — like this." And he kissed her flush on the mouth.

Even as Joe relished the sweet contact, his feverish brain screamed a warning that he had jumped headlong into a cactus patch. He didn't linger but a second or two, fearful Raylene would start to fight and push him away. He broke off the contact and took a step back, his chin held high, cheek exposed, ready to receive the slap that would surely come.

To both his shock and relief, Raylene didn't strike him. Instead, she gazed at him with an odd sort of scrutiny. Subtly, her pink tongue traced a delicate path along her lips, then she also took a step back.

"Mrs. Lawson had some fryers at the store, so I bought one to prepare for supper." Her words were so matter-of-fact, Joe about sat down from shock. "You've probably noticed I'm not a great cook," she continued, "but I do make pretty good fried chicken."

"It's my favorite meal." Joe mumbled his dumbfounded response.

Raylene gave a nod of her head. "I'll get started on supper then." And, with that said, she rotated and walked to the kitchen.

Joe stared after her until the door to the living quarters closed. Of any reaction he might have expected from kissing Raylene, her pretending nothing had happened was not even on the list. After the passing of a few mind-numbing seconds, he stared blankly up at the ceiling.

"Okay, Lord, You got me stumped." He sighed in defeat. "I ain't got a clue as to how to play this hand." He grunted. "Fact is, I ain't even sure who's dealing the cards!"

"It means something," Chase growled. "That judge took me for over a hundred bucks. What kind of judge plays cards like that?"

Vern gave a shake of his head. "You just had an off night, Chase. I've never won when you sat at my table. Fact be told, I don't 'member you ever losing more than a few bucks."

Chase stared hard at the big man. "What happened to your idea of beating the guy into dog meat? Have you forgotten how he blindsided you with a pistol?"

"The judge told me straight out he could never beat me in a fight." Vern excused his lack of retribution. "Conking me alongside the head was the only thing he could do, other than shoot me dead."

Chase exploded at the logic. "You've got rocks in your head!"

"Bulldog's got it right, Chase." Keno sided with Vern. "The judge has been nothing but square. We told you how he handled Wade Lewis and his boys. Hell, them fellows were thanking him by the time they left town, as if he had done them a favor."

Chase threw his hands up into the air. "I'm surrounded by slack-brained idiots!"

Keno extended an arm and pointed a menacing finger at Chase. "You'd best rein in your tongue, sonny boy. It's your brother who casts the tall shadow around here, not you. If we was to tell him you were skimming an extra ten percent in taxes, he'd toss you out of town with nothing but a kick to the seat of your pants."

"Dunn's backbone has turned to mush since he married Myra," Chase fired back. "He's willing to let our operation go to the devil and do nothing about it."

"We've had our say, Chase," Keno retorted. "We ain't gonna run the judge out of town — not unless Dunn gives the order himself."

"Keno's telling it straight," Vern agreed.

Rather than take a whip to a dead mule, Chase spun on his heel and left the two men behind him. He pounded the dust with his stomping feet, filled with a helpless rage. The whole bunch of them were aboard a train headed to hell, and no one was even trying to put on the brakes.

"Damn that Myra!" he muttered. "She's

the one who caused all this. She turned Dunn into a whimpering puppy and joined ranks with the new judge." That woman would be the ruination of everything he and Dunn had built up in Gold Butte.

Chase decided he needed a place to think. Dunn had a shady porch and a couple of comfortable chairs. He would plop down and ponder on a way to turn this situation around. He had to do something before the judge confronted Dunn about the high taxes. He and Pike had a good thing going here. It wouldn't do for some snoopy do-gooder to become involved. If Dunn learned the truth, he would do as Keno said and boot him and Pike both out of town. Somehow, he had to figure out how to get rid of that damn judge.

Joe had still not gotten an answer from Raylene about the election. He had made up his mind, but it would be a plus to have her support his idea. They had finished supper, and it was growing dark when he decided it was time to start the roulette wheel spinning.

"I'll be back in a while, ma'am," he said, picking up his hat.

"Joe" — she sighed emphatically — "the name is Raylene."

"Yeah, but it still don't come easy."

She put on a stern look. "I let you kiss me, Joe. Doesn't that mean anything?"

He stood frozen to the ground. "You . . . let . . . me?"

"Did I resist?" she challenged. "Did I slap your face for being impulsive or impertinent?"

"No, but I figured it was because you were too polite, too much a lady to react."

"Not at all," she disagreed. "I *allowed* you to kiss me." She stated it as a fact. "That makes us more than mere acquaintances, and as such, it is an insult for you to call me *ma'am.* Do you wish to insult me?"

"No, ma—" He caught himself and corrected his speech. "Raylene," he finished, "I would never intentionally insult you."

"Then you will call me Raylene from now on. Agreed?"

Joe moved closer and met her mesmerizing stare. Flecks of gold glistened in the dim light as if there were an intense fire burning in her eyes. He was drawn toward her as if by a magnetic pull. He would have kissed her except for the fact that she took a step back.

"Joe!" she said sharply but under her breath. "I didn't say you could do it again — not right this minute."

He frowned. "But . . ."

"Didn't you say you had something to do?" she asked him.

"I'm guessing it could wait a spell."

Raylene rotated her head from side to side. "I think you'd better get on with whatever it is. I'm feeling a little vulnerable at the moment. I need some time to recover my good sense."

Joe sighed. "You females are a confusing sort. Every time I make a step in your direction, I feel like I'm playing a new game where I don't know the rules."

"With a woman, Joe," Raylene replied, "there are no rules. Each of us is a little different from all of the rest. It's part of our appeal."

"Now I commence to see why I took up gambling, rather than trying to understand women."

"I've got some laundry to do." Raylene changed the subject. "Would you like me to wash your dirty clothes too?"

Joe wondered if the offer had a secondary meaning. Raylene had not offered to do his laundry since the first day they were in town. Was this one of those strange rules she had mentioned?

"Uh, maybe next time . . . Raylene. I left my duds over at the Spanish lady's place.

With three kids to raise, she needs the business."

"You continue to amaze me by what a thoughtful, generous man you are, Joe."

"Yeah" was the only thing he could think of to say.

"Be sure you're back in time for the fried chicken."

"Yeah," Joe said a second time, wondering what had happened to his power of speech. Durned if Raylene's logic hadn't fogged his brain. He was about as confused as a fly in a spider web. *And near as helpless!* he added mentally.

CHAPTER TWELVE

Joe spied Chase sitting on the porch of Dunn's two-story house. The man got to his feet at Joe's approach and stepped forward to block his path.

"What do you want, Judge?" Estcott demanded to know.

"I've come to have a talk with your brother," Joe told him.

"My brother is a busy man. Why don't you tell me what you're after?"

Joe took a moment to evaluate Chase. He tried to determine how much force the man was willing to use to stop him. After a short span of time, he relaxed his posture.

"I need to speak to him about the upcoming fall festival," he said casually, "to raise money for civic improvements."

Chase pulled a face. "Civic improvements?"

"The streets need to be kept clean, we need to build more walkways for the wet season — that sort of thing."

Chase turned his head and spat a stream of tobacco juice onto the dusty street. "I think you're lying to me, Judge. I know you've been asking a lot of questions lately, and I seen you stop by and talk to Steve at the newspaper. You thinking of putting an ad in the paper to try and drum up more business or something?"

"Would you like to tell your brother I'm here?" Joe ignored the question. "Or do I have to go through you?"

Chase put his hand on the butt of his gun. "I'm not as easy to surprise as Bulldog, Judge."

Joe smiled. "I hope you're handier with a gun than you are at cards."

Chase set his teeth together hard and bore into Joe with a smoldering gaze. "I'm going to find out who you really are, Judge. You can count on that."

"You'll be doing me a real favor there, Chase. I mean it."

"Judge Stanfield!" It was Myra. She stepped into the doorway and smiled at him. "How nice of you to pay us a visit." She threw a hard glance at Chase. "Is there something you need here at the house, Chase?"

The man's glare was vehement, but his

voice was respectful. "I was just making use of your porch, Myra. As for me and the judge here, we was just passing the time about the weather." He touched the brim of his hat in a salute and put a hard look on Joe. "See you later, Judge." Then he left the porch and walked away.

Once he had moved down the street, Myra regarded Joe with a curious perusal. "Is that what you two were doing just now, speaking about the weather?"

Joe grinned. "That's one way of looking at it. We was commencing to see if there was going to be a storm right here on your porch."

"Did you come here to criticize or give my husband a hard time?"

"I was planning on it being more of a discussion and sharing of information, Mrs. Estcott."

She hesitated a moment. "You should know that some people around here don't believe you are who you claim to be."

"I aim to settle that question for everyone concerned in a few days."

Myra showed an interest but did not pursue his remark. "I should also remind you that I am bound to support my husband's decision. Whatever the project or idea you have in mind, I stand with Dunn on the issue."

Joe gave her another smile. "That's as it should be, Mrs. Estcott. A man and his wife should always make their decisions together and support each other."

"This way," she said, obviously satisfied. They passed through the sitting room and the kitchen. A sizable office was next to a bedroom. Dunn and another man were sitting on opposite sides of a large desk. It appeared the two of them were examining a ledger together.

"Dunn" — Myra interrupted their work — "Judge Stanfield would like a few moments of your time. I hope you don't mind that I brought him to you."

"Not at all, Myra honey," he said amiably, while regarding Joe with an inquisitive gaze. "What can we do for you, Judge?"

Joe stepped into the office and got right to business. "I wanted to tell you that there will be an election next Saturday."

Dunn maintained an outward serenity. "What kind of election?"

Joe removed a folded sheet of paper from his pocket, opened it flat, and laid it on the desk for the man to read.

"An election for both sheriff and judge?" Dunn asked in wonder.

Joe gave a nod. "A judge can be voted out

of office, same as your sheriff."

"Chase brought in Pike Unger to be acting sheriff," he replied.

"Exactly," Joe agreed. "*Acting* sheriff. However, the law states that a county sheriff can be elected or removed from his position by the people within that county."

"It says on your bulletin that a United States Marshal will be here to oversee this election?"

"In case anyone decides they don't like the outcome," Joe told him. "When the audit starts, there might be some outcry, if we didn't do it legal and all."

"Audit?"

"The tax expenses here are double what I've ever seen in any other town. The US Marshal will be here to arrest anyone who has been defrauding the businesses or citizens."

"Our taxes support the local law and city government. Any excess of funds has been set aside to build a school for the children of Gold Butte."

"Won't be any children if you keep fleecing the people at the rate of twenty percent."

Dunn frowned. "You've obviously gotten some misinformation. We don't charge twenty percent, and I have no concerns about an audit. My accountant and I will gladly open our records for an auditor's inspection."

"I wanted you to know what I was doing, Dunn," Joe told him, a bit surprised that the man didn't seem aware of the high rate of tax. With that notion in mind, he took a more comfortable stance. "You have a wonderful wife, and I think you're an all right guy. My main reason for coming here was to advise you of what was going on. I intend to do all of this legal-like and don't want any trouble with the election."

"My brother and Sheriff Unger may oppose the election," Dunn admitted. "But I can assure you, I have no objections."

Joe thanked him, said good-bye, and left the house. He wondered a second time at Dunn's curious frown when he mentioned the taxes. Perhaps he was not in charge of that end of things. The fact that he would not oppose the election was a plus. He would have to deal with Unger and Chase, but he figured he was up to the chore.

Chase could not believe what his brother was saying. "You mean you're gonna let him do it?" he cried. "You're gonna let him have an election?"

"I'm not a tyrant, Chase. I don't intend to oppose the will of the people. Besides" —

he uttered a grunt — "who is going to run against Pike Unger?"

"The man must have someone lined up."

"Look at the ad he is placing," Dunn invited, spreading the sheet of paper on the desktop.

NOTICE OF SPECIAL ELECTION

All legal voters (men over the age of 21 who reside within the Gold Butte boundaries) are requested to register at Lawson's Mercantile prior to Friday night. The voting will be on Saturday and will be supervised by US Marshal Hoyt Cahill. This election is to appoint or confirm the office of both County Sheriff and the Judgeship of Gold Butte. Nominees for sheriff are Pike Unger and Anonymous. The judge to be confirmed or ousted is Mr Stanfield.

"He can't do this!" Chase cried. "And what the hell is a vote for Anonymous?"

"I'd say it is a vote against Pike," Dunn replied. "Likely the US Marshal will appoint a temporary sheriff if Pike gets voted out."

"What?" Chase was incredulous. "They can do that? They can vote for nobody?"

"I've never heard of it before, but they

might be holding back the name until the day of the election to prevent anyone from threatening or trying to harm the new nominee."

"What are we going to do about it?"

"I'm not going to do anything about it, Chase. The US Marshal is involved. And we've been up-front all along. We have nothing to fear from an audit."

Chase paled at the news. "An audit?"

"The judge has the mistaken idea we are charging a twenty percent tax. I don't know where he got his information, but nothing more will come of it unless the people elect a new sheriff."

"I knew that judge was trouble!"

"If I were you, I'd tell Pike to start campaigning. Have him point out the good things about our town. We haven't had a murder here since he took over. Fact is, the only killing was the bounty hunter the judge killed. Encourage the people to support him, especially in light of the fact that they don't even know who he's running against."

Chase stared at Dunn as if he had been possessed. "The taters has sure enough slid off of your plate, Dunn! You ain't thinking with your head no more; you're being led around like a worn-out nag!"

"Look, Chase" — Dunn had reached his

limit for tolerance — "I'm not going to debate the issue. If you don't like the way I run things, you can pull up stakes and try your hand at doing some real work for a living."

"This is that judge's doing!" Chase wailed. "Well, you're gonna see that I've been right about him. I wrote a letter to the state and asked some pointed questions about Gordon Stanfield, the son." Chase waited for the news to sink in. "And when word comes back that he's a fake, you're gonna be the one who looks like a cow stuck up to its belly in a bog, not me."

Dunn didn't reply to his brother's outburst but watched him storm from the room.

As the door slammed behind Chase, Myra came into the room and stood next to him. "I didn't intend to eavesdrop, but I heard most of your conversation with Chase."

"Could mean trouble for the judge — him writing a letter."

Myra bit her lower lip. "If Gordon isn't a real judge, it would have come out sooner or later anyway . . . especially in light of the election."

Dunn looked into her eyes. "So you approve of my actions on this?"

"I always knew you were a good man,

Dunn," she said quietly, smiling at him. "Even when you allowed Chase and Pike to run off those other two judges, I was sure you had a good reason."

"I didn't want them to ruin our life here," Dunn replied. "If they had been the kind of reformers to form a union and possibly bring about a strike, we could have gone broke. With the low-grade ore we've been into lately, a work stoppage for two or three weeks would have caused more financial damage than we could absorb."

She looked him squarely in the eye. "You know, Dunn, the reason I married you wasn't only because you had money and ambition. I always knew you were the kind of man I could respect."

"Respect?" he repeated. "I allowed those other two judges to be run out of town!"

"You were probably right about them. They might have been radical rabble-rousers or holier-than-thou crusaders. If so, they wouldn't have wanted to unite the people of our town for goodness' sake; they would have pitted us against one another for their own personal gain, to make a name for themselves."

"And you don't believe Gordon Stanfield is that sort?"

She giggled at the notion. "The judge —

whether he is genuine or counterfeit —
wants a better life for everyone in Gold
Butte. I believe he thinks the best path we
can take is to work together."

Dunn slipped an arm around Myra's
waist. To his delight, she turned to meet his
advance. They stood as if dancing, gazing
into each other's eyes.

"I always figured my age was a disadvan-
tage in our relationship, Myra honey. I
mean, you could have chosen from a number of men your own age."

"You were the mature sort of man I was
looking to marry, Dunn. I chose you because you were stable and already estab-
lished. We both got what we wanted."

"All I ever really wanted was your love."
He gave a careless shrug of one shoulder.
"Although I would have enjoyed watching
you be a mother too."

She rose up on tiptoe and kissed him.
When she pulled back, she smiled. "Like I
said, we both got what we wanted."

It took a moment for that to sink in. "You
mean . . ." At her nod, he responded with a
wide smile of his own. "Now I've got more
than I ever could have hoped for."

They laughed together, hugged, and began
to dance merrily about the room. The only
music was their mutual happiness, but they

were completely in step with each other.

It was well after dark when Myra entered the courtroom and spied Raylene busy polishing the new desk. The woman paused from her work and offered a smile of greeting.

"Hello, Myra," she greeted her. "I've been meaning to thank you for buying a desk and chairs for our courtroom. Once we have the platform built, it will look as official as any in the state."

Myra looked past Raylene. "Isn't the judge here?" she asked.

"He's over at the Palace. He said he was going to socialize so he could talk up the election." She smiled, "If I were a betting person, I'd wager he's playing cards."

Myra remained sober. "I'm afraid there might be some trouble coming."

The smile left Raylene's face. "What is it?"

Myra stared at the floor, unable to meet Raylene's questioning stare. "I learned today that Chase has sent off a letter — I don't know when, but I believe it's been a few days."

"A letter?" Raylene repeated.

Myra clarified the report. "Chase suspects that your brother is not who he claims to be. He wrote a letter of inquiry to the state office about him."

Raylene uttered a groan of defeat. "I can't say I'm surprised."

"Should we be concerned about this?" Myra asked, reading the worry in Raylene's expression. "Is Gordon your brother? Is he a real judge?"

Raylene refused to look at her, so Myra moved over and seized hold of her hand. "You have to tell me the truth," she coaxed. "Maybe Dunn and I can do something to help."

It took a moment, but then Raylene sat down on a bench. Without further cajoling, she blurted out the truth. Myra listened as she explained how Joe had come to her aid, how she had covered for him with the posse, and the way she had coerced him into taking the job as judge. When she finished, Myra remained calmly sympathetic.

"I watched you when Gordon was presiding over the court, standing at the pulpit, Raylene," Myra said. "I saw you flinch and gasp, even smother a laugh at his handling of the proceedings. Mostly, though, I could see how proud you were of Gordon."

"His name is Joe, and I was not aware that I was so transparent."

"Some things are easy to see," Myra said.

"Like the fact that Gordon — *Joe,*" she corrected, "is hopelessly in love with you."

The words struck Raylene like a bucket of ice water. She stared at Myra and rotated her head back and forth. "You . . . you can see that?"

Myra laughed. "A blind person would see it, Raylene. Joe is so blatantly obvious — it's in his voice, his eyes, his every action when he's around you."

Raylene returned to the problem at hand. "They are certain to send someone from the state to investigate. They know by this time that Joe is an impostor."

"What are you going to do?"

"Like everything else that has happened since I met Joe, I believe he is a step ahead of everyone else. I think Joe set up this election to end our charade." Raylene sighed. "I don't know his whole plan, but a judge can be appointed or elected to office, regardless of his qualifications."

Myra bobbed her head in agreement. "What about the job of sheriff? Who did he pick to run against Pike Unger?"

"He won't tell me, but I'm sure he has it all worked out. He uses his gambling skills in everything he does. You can bet he has this all planned out to the last poker chip."

Myra laughed. "You're starting to sound

like him."

Raylene smiled. "Yes, I am constantly amazed at some of the things he says and does. He has no training; he simply uses common sense and relates to people on their own level."

"I thought I should warn you about the letter so you and Joe can decide on a plan of action," Myra told her. Displaying a smile, she added, "Or maybe he can factor it into his gambling mentality."

Raylene laughed. "I — we — appreciate the warning. I'll be sure to tell Joe."

Myra said good-bye and left the courthouse. It was cool and dark outside, and rather than walk past the saloon, Myra kept to the opposite side of the street. She had only gone a short way when a shadow popped out of the darkness and blocked her path.

Myra sucked in her breath and froze in her tracks. She started to cry out, but the phantom sprang upon her and clamped a brutal hand over her mouth. She immediately began to struggle against the man, but he was much stronger then she. He dragged her down the alleyway and roughly slammed her up against the wall of the building. Myra was held there, terrified, as a shadowy face appeared inches from her own.

"You just had to get in the middle!" Chase's voice hissed, his whiskey-foul breath right in her face. "You've been asking for a mind-your-own-business lesson ever since your latched on to my brother!"

Myra ceased her fighting, hoping a submissive posture would cause Chase to lessen his hold. He did remove his hand from her mouth, but only to clench her about the throat. She was pinned tightly, trapped by his forearm pressed to her chest and his body firmly planted against her own. In such a position, she was unable to put up any resistance. Moreover, he had only to squeeze his fingers, and she would strangle for want of air.

"You ruined everything, you backstabbing witch!" Chase ranted. "You took my brother and turned him into your personal slave."

Myra fearfully turned her head from side to side, but the hand about her neck tightened. She managed a constricted swallow, her chest heaving from exertion, but she could no longer draw adequate air into her lungs. Terror entered her heart, an icy fear that she would never take another breath.

CHAPTER THIRTEEN

Myra was barely clinging to consciousness, seeking the strength to fight back. A blackness threatened to engulf her brain, she gagged for want of air —

Chase suddenly released his hold, and she collapsed, sitting down abruptly. She sucked in gulps of air, feverishly fighting to regain her wind. When she raised her eyes, she saw that there were now two men in the passageway. One was pummeling the other, punching him with flying fists that made a sickening *smack* with each contact.

Chase buckled from the violent onslaught and landed on his stomach at Myra's feet. At that moment she did the first unladylike act she could remember. She struck out with one foot and kicked him alongside the head.

Strong hands gripped her by the arms, and she was lifted to her feet.

"Ma'am?" She recognized the judge's

263

voice. "Are you all right?"

Myra not only managed to stand, she threw both arms around Joe's neck, buried her face against his chest, and clung to him.

Joe was stunned. "Mrs. Estcott?"

She did not respond but held on tightly for several long seconds. After a short time she recovered enough to pull back.

"Joe — Judge!" Her entire body was trembling. "How . . . ?" She sniffed back the tears that filled her eyes. "Where did you come from?"

"You called me *Joe?*"

"Raylene told me everything."

"I was just leaving the saloon, and I seen a woman being pulled off of the street," he explained. "I would have gotten here sooner, but I thought it might have been a couple of lovers stealing a kiss or two."

Myra gave Chase a sharp glance. "Can we m-move away from him?" Her voice was quavering. "I — I don't want him to wake up, and . . ."

No other words were necessary. Joe escorted her to the street and began to walk her home.

"Did he hurt you?"

"He throttled me — I nearly blacked out."

"The dirty, stinkin' maggot! I ought to go back and break both of his arms."

"I believe you dished out enough punishment that he will remember it for days to come," she replied.

Joe chuckled. "With luck, he'll even feel that love tap you gave him for a spell."

"I'm likely the only girl to ever attend Vassar College who kicked a man when he was down," she said, a lightness entering her voice for the first time.

"Your reputation is safe with me," Joe teased, "but it would be best not to make a habit of it."

"Joe, I would rather not tell Dunn about this," Myra whispered after they had gone a short way. "Can we keep this . . . incident between us?"

"If that's the way you want it," Joe promised.

"It's obvious Chase was staggering drunk. Otherwise, he never would have dared touch me."

"I seen a bottle fall out of his pocket during the fight," Joe said. "But being drunk ain't no excuse for what he did."

"I don't wish to come between Dunn and Chase," Myra said. "They were very close until I came into the picture."

"It's clear Dunn became a whole lot better man, whilst Chase still ain't worth spit."

"But you do understand?"

"Like I said, ma'am, whatever you say is how we'll play the game."

They stopped at the doorway to the Estcott residence. Myra held Joe's hand for a long moment, smiling at him.

"Whatever happens in the future, Joe," she murmured sincerely, "I'll always think of you as the most special judge I've ever known."

Joe was too dumbfounded to speak. He waited until Myra entered the house, and then he turned back for the courthouse. He wasn't so confused that he didn't keep an eye out for Chase. He warily returned along the street with his hand resting on the butt of his gun. It would only take an instant to bring the weapon to bear.

When he reached the alley, he gave it a long look. However, Chase was gone. Joe had given the man a good pounding, so he had probably crawled off to lick his wounds.

When Joe reached the courthouse, he entered to find Raylene pacing the floor. When she told him about Myra's warning, he shrugged it off.

"What are we going to do?" Raylene asked anxiously. "If they send someone from the State Department here, he is going to want to know who you really are!"

"The election will settle everything," Joe

told her. "You wait and see."

"What about a sheriff? Who is the anonymous candidate?"

"It's nothing you have to worry about, Raylene. Trust me, I've got all the bets covered."

She didn't question him further. Instead, a sensuous smile played along her lips. "I wouldn't have believed you when we first met, Joe, but I've come to think you are the most able man I've ever known. I'm certain my father would have liked you."

"Truth be told," Joe replied, "you're the only one I ever wanted to please."

Raylene displayed a playful mien. "You mean so you could repay your debt to me."

"The debt be hanged!" Joe countered at once. "I was taken with you from the start, lady. I've done what I could for these people, 'cause they are good and decent people, and I wanted to help. But acting the part of a judge and doing all the pretending was for you alone."

"I'm flattered, Joe," she said softly. "And I will trust to your judgment."

Joe grinned. "I'll try to make you proud."

"You've already done that, Joe," she murmured. Then she leaned over and kissed him sweetly, with the warmth of a woman in love.

■ ■ ■ ■

Marshal Cahill arrived early Saturday morning. He was no taller than Joe, but he had a bit more girth and a touch of gray at his ears. He shook hands with Joe and Tom, and the three of them set about checking the registrations of all the voters. Tom had closed the store for the day so the voting could take place. He set up a table on the front porch with two chairs for himself and the marshal. Tom would find each man's name on the voting register, and Cahill would hand the man a ballot. It was a simple piece of paper with a box to mark either for Sheriff Unger or Anonymous and a Yes or No box to confirm or oust the judge. As the men began to line up to cast their votes, Tom and Cahill were ready to proceed.

"I don't know no one named Anonymous," the first man in line complained. "How do I know who to vote for?"

"It's simple enough," Cahill told him. "A vote for Anonymous is a vote against Sheriff Unger."

"The hell you say!" the man exclaimed. Turning his head, he spoke to those in line behind him. "Vote for Anonymous, fellows.

If he wins, Sheriff Unger is out on his big, fat hindquarters!"

It took the better part of the day for every man to cast his vote. Next, the marshal and Tom moved their station inside the store and proceeded to count the votes. It was nearly dusk when the two of them stepped out onto the mercantile porch to announce the results. It appeared nearly everyone in town and many from miles around had come to hear the outcome.

"The voting has been tabulated." Tom quieted the crowd with his statement. "Marshal Cahill will give you the tally and explain the results."

Cahill possessed a strong voice. He used it to reach everyone within hearing distance.

"Those voting in favor of Sheriff Unger — fourteen," he said. "Those voting against Sheriff Unger — ninety-six."

A shout of approval went up from the crowd.

"On the matter of the judgeship, the count was three opposed and a hundred and seven in favor." He allowed a second cheer but then held up a hand to quiet the crowd. "There are a couple of points that must be clarified here. Please hold down the noise until I finish."

Once quiet had been restored, Cahill nodded in Joe's direction. "This man here, the one calling himself Gordon Stanfield, is actually Joe Bratt. He assumed temporary judgeship here in Gold Butte while requesting an inquiry into a charge of murder in the town of Pueblo. Upon review of the case and after all depositions were taken, it was determined that no crime had been committed. The ruling on Joe's shooting a man was self-defense." Cahill let the news sink in.

"The man he killed within this township, known only as Taggart, was a bounty hunter hired by Conroy Masterson, who has since pleaded guilty to hiring him and has been sentenced to prison. That settled, I should now inform you that the new sheriff of Gold Butte is Joe Bratt."

The chatter and questions erupted from a hundred voices at once. Cahill let them go on for a few moments before he lifted his hands again for silence.

"If Joe is the new sheriff," Tom asked, obviously as stumped as everyone else, "what about the judgeship?"

"There was a minor misprint on the ballot," Cahill explained.

Tom frowned and pointed to one of the official pieces of paper. "It says Mr. Stanfield, but we all thought Joe Bratt was

Stanfield."

Cahill gave his head a negative shake. "Not *Mr.* Stanfield. There was a minor misprint in that the *M* and *R* should have been separated by a space. The new judge of Gold Butte is Miss Mary Raylene Stanfield!"

The news circulated for a few mind-numbing seconds of sinking in, and then a miner cried out, "Shore! I'd vote for her!"

Another man looked at him as if he had the common sense of a weed. "You *did* vote for her, dummy!"

"She handled the Boggs case like a veteran lawyer," sounded off a third man.

"Made that high-priced Lavar Crump look the fool, she did," added a nearby woman.

Joe stepped up in front of the men. "You good people ought to know the whole truth," he announced. "Miss Stanfield is the one who has dealt with *all* the legal claims made to the court. I have simply ruled the way she decided. She has been doing the job of judge here for most ever since we arrived."

Cahill again took the floor. "Joe sent letters to the governor and my office to set all of this into motion. Miss Stanfield has the necessary training and education to hold

271

the position, and the governor himself has decreed that she can accept the appointment. As of this minute, Raylene Stanfield is an official Justice of the Peace for the state of Colorado. Other than for a mining town in Wyoming, she is the first woman I know of to hold such a position in the country."

Joe waited until the cheers died down. Then he pointed up the street. The crowd looked in that direction and saw that Keno and Vern had two men shackled in chains — Chase Estcott and Pike Unger. As they approached the gathering, Dunn left Myra's side to confront his brother. He stopped suddenly when he spied the bruises and swelling about his face.

"What the hell, Chase?"

"I wouldn't have really hurt her none, big brother," he whined. "Honest! I only wanted to throw a scare into Myra."

Dunn staggered back as if he had been sucker-punched. "Myra?"

"I mean it, Dunn!" Chase cried. "Even if the judge hadn't come along, I never would have hurt her none."

Dunn spun and stared at Myra. She lowered her head, displaying guilt for not having told him. He whirled back on Chase. "You attacked Myra? How could you do that?"

"I'd been drinking, Dunn. I wasn't thinking straight." He tried to raise his hand to point, but the iron bracelets prevented such action. "See? She ain't hurt none! She's just fine!"

"The bruises on her neck!" Dunn exploded. "I couldn't imagine how she had gotten those marks from her scarf getting caught in the door. You tried to strangle her!"

"Dunn," he pleaded, "it was all a mistake, and nothing happened. She's fine, and I got a thorough thrashing for grabbing her. You've got to help me!"

"Like you helped yourself to a ten percent tax?" he roared. "You and Unger have been collecting twice as much tax as we agreed upon. Damn you, Chase. I hope they lock you up and never let you out!"

Chase was next to tears. "Dunn, you can't let them take me to jail. I only wanted to get enough money to live the good life, to be more like you."

"You never wanted to work for anything, Chase. Now I find you were defrauding these people and taking the bread off the tables of the miners and their families." Dunn's chest heaved with his resolve. "You attacked my wife and could have killed her and our unborn child."

"Child?" Chase whimpered. "I didn't know nothing about Myra being with child."

"I hope you rot in prison, Chase," Dunn said thickly. "And don't you ever show up around here again. If you do, I'll see you are charged with trying to kill my wife."

"Take them to jail," Joe ordered Keno. "You and Vern are still on the payroll as deputies, unless I discover you were involved in taking some of the extra tax money."

Keno shook his head. "We told you straight, Judge — uh, Sheriff. Pike and Chase warned us to keep our mouths shut, but we didn't get one dime more than our pay."

Dunn spoke up again. "My accountant will begin an audit tomorrow, Sheriff Bratt. We will discover how much my brother and the sheriff stole from the people of Gold Butte. When we know the full amount, I will see that every dollar is returned to the businessmen, even if it takes me a year to pay it back. Then we will sit down and reexamine the current tax structure and figure a reasonable sum for the future. I'm confident the price of every item and service in town will go down by no less than ten percent."

A hearty cheer arose from the throats of everyone — save Chase and Unger.

Cahill shook hands with Joe once the crowd began to dissipate. "I believe this is going to be a fine town, Sheriff Bratt."

"We've a lot of good people here, Marshal."

"I will oversee Dunn and his accountant so I can examine the tax records. We'll clear up this tax business, and I'll be out of your way in a couple days." He grinned. "As a bonus, I'll escort the two prisoners to jail on my return trip."

Dunn came over to shake Joe's hand. "I'm damn sorry about all this, Judge — I mean, Sheriff Bratt. It's my fault. I was too preoccupied with my other business ventures to notice that my own brother was a crook."

Myra moved up to stand at Dunn's side. Her arm naturally locked through his, and she smiled at Joe.

"You did a fine job as a judge, Joe," she said. "I know you'll do a good job as sheriff."

"Thank you, ma'am."

"And I want to thank you for your advice. My folks want to come visit" — she gave a beaming smile — "as soon as the baby is here."

He smiled at the news. "I'm glad you wrote to them."

Myra laughed. "Actually, I couldn't wait

for the mail. I sent them a wire, and they answered the very next day. If you hadn't convinced me, I never would have reached out to them."

"The love of a parent," Joe reminded her.

"Yes," she replied, "the devotion of loving parents."

Raylene joined Joe after working her way through a host of well-wishers — a good many of them women.

"You might have warned me," she scolded Joe. "I had no idea you had written the governor."

"Looks as if your first case will be Chase and Unger for fraud or whatever the legal term is for collecting their own taxes."

"I believe an eighteen-month sentence would be fair and just — providing the two men turn over all their funds and possessions to the court. We will then refund as much money as we can to the business owners, and Dunn claims he will make up the difference. I'm glad the stores and businesses can pass along the savings to the miners and ranchers."

"Sounds fine," Joe said.

"And we'll do our own audits after this to make certain the taxes are used only for town expenditures," she outlined. "We're going to need a school, perhaps a water wagon with a pump, in case of fire, and I would like —"

"Hold back the team, Judge," Joe teased. "You ain't been in office five minutes, and you're already changing the world."

Raylene laughed. "I guess we can take things one step at a time."

"I believe you've got yourself a real judge," Cahill told Joe.

"No, Marshal, I've got myself a future bride."

Raylene didn't say a word. Instead, she stepped forward and kissed him. The act came as a surprise, but Joe relished the incredible tenderness of her kiss. He didn't know what he had said to induce such a show of emotion, but it was the most delightful experience he had ever known.

ABOUT THE AUTHOR

Terrell L. Bowers sometimes thinks he was born with boots and spurs. His father was his inspiration. He provided Terrell with his own horse and cows to ride and rope. Whether on small acre lots or fair-sized farms, he always had a horse and rope handy. Terrell shared his father's enthusiasm for westerns and grew up rooting for Bob Steele, Johnny Mack Brown, Roy Rogers, and John Wayne. Western blood is in his veins, and he loves to create a new story with new characters and then let his imagination run wild. "Fortunately," Terrell writes, "I have a beautiful, loving wife and two angelic girls, who understand and accept my endless hours at a typewriter. My principal desire is that somewhere there are western lovers who find my stories entertaining."

Terrell is the author of many westerns for AVALON.